JERSEY'S UNEXPECTED ARRIVAL

Written by

Tami L. Colby

ISBN: 978-1-7376174-0-2 (paperback)

Acknowledgement

I want to thank the following people who have helped make Annie Jones And The Animal Sanctuary Part Two, Jersey's Unexpected Arrival, possible.

Robert St. Andrews Editor: Thank you for your time, talent, and dedication.

Thank you to my friends, my family, my children: Kristina Hart, Kiera Kennedy, Alexander Colby, and Adam Colby- Without your love, support, encouragement, I wouldn't be on this journey.

A big Thank you to the following people below for allowing your pup to be a part of the cover.

Manon Cote and Molly Thank you, Manon, for allowing Molly to be a part of the Annie Jones story again.

Lisa Roces Mennella and Jersey Thank you so much for allowing Jersey to be a part of Annie's story.

Heather Simpson and Rubble

Amanda Sabatini and Lexus

Kiera Kennedy and Kenzie

Connie Horton and Bella

Jill Holland and Daphne

Kaylee Hulsaver and Harlow
Dan Ashcroft and Sprocket

And last but certainly not least,

Kiki Mc Gough and Watson:
*Watson is an inspiration to us all. He is not aware that he is different from the other dogs, and although he gets around on wheels rather well, I would say, the smile on his face says it all. His happy approach to life and what it has to offer him is remarkable. *
Watson's photo -Furever Friends Pet Photography

Introduction

Annie struggled to make sense of what her gut was trying to tell her. It was not part of the plan.

"I am taking the farm off the market Ralph—this town needs me here!" Annie felt a twinge in her stomach. She knew she had made the statement in haste. Annie's life was in turmoil. She had turned down Sam's marriage proposal which had caused a lot of friction between the two. Annie loved Sam but marriage was a big step for the both of them. She knew Sam's ego had been wounded, but she was seeing the practical side of it. *We had never even had a romantic kiss.* But Annie wanted a life with Sam, she wanted this life and saving that dog's life reminded her of why she moved to Murphy. Sam wasn't without his own feelings. He was thankful to be staying with Annie in Murphy, but so many questions were still left unanswered.

Was it possible for the two of them to live here as just friends? This was different from their apartment in New York; this was Annie's house. She was the owner, and like it or not, that changed everything.

Sam wanted to marry Annie and was still licking his wounds from her rejection. He was now forced to face the reality that she may never agree to marry him. He had to decide if his friendship with Annie was worth giving up his life in New York. Murphy was where he wanted to be before the proposal. Now, as a single man, Sam felt differently There were no clubs to go to, no shopping malls and only one coffee shop in town. He presumed most folks in Murphy met their sweethearts in high school and then married. In the back of his mind, he was haunted by the words, *this is not your house, and if Annie decides she does not want you here, you will have no place to go.* Sam reminisced about the life Annie, and he had shared for so many years. She was his best friend, and he loved her, but was he willing to just be a roommate? Was he willing to give up his life in New York with the hopes that one day she will change her mind and see him as more than a roommate or best friend?

Characters

Molly- Annie's Puggle
Sam- Annie's best friend
Annie - Main character
Rose- Annie's mom
Ben - Annie's dad
Kristina- Flight attendant
Brian- Annie's brother
Sally- Roommate from college
Joe- The local veterinarian
Chet- Sam's old client/ friend
Jolene- Chet's wife
Joe- The apartment manager
Kevin- Sam's friend
Kate- Kevin's wife
Julee- Kevin's sister
Jersey- Julee's Puggle
Albert- Pub Owner
Matthew Stevens- Photographer
Tom- Sally's ex-husband
Pammi- Neighbor who is pregnant

Sean- Pammi's husband
Eileen- Neighbor
Isaac- Sam's artist friend
Peggy- Julee Head Nurse
Aleena- Annie's coworker

Contents

CHAPTER 1

The Elephant in the Room

Sam was on the phone with his boss when Annie walked into the kitchen. She made herself a cup of coffee and sat down at the table. The past few weeks had been less than comfortable. There was an elephant in the room that neither one of them cared to confront, at least not anytime soon. Molly could sense the tension. She was fidgeting with her toys more than usual. Annie carried her to the kitchen to help settle her down.

"Come on, Molly, let's get you something to eat while daddy finishes his phone call." *Isn't it funny that I see Sam as Molly's daddy, and yet I just couldn't accept his marriage proposal? I am not sure if it was the fear of marriage that held me back or the fact that we had never been romantic. Up until these past few weeks, I never imagined being married to Sam.*

Sam hung up the phone, grabbed his coffee, and sat down. Annie could feel his eyes glaring down at her while she prepared Molly's breakfast. Molly was still the Diva she had always been, and homemade-gourmet food was all she would eat. Annie smiled as she thought of her Uncle Jack. *He knew Molly was the perfect fit for Annie, or perhaps the opposite was true.* Annie knew they were perfect for one another. "Thank you, Uncle Jack."

Sam interrupted Annie's thoughts. "Annie, we need to schedule a trip back to New York so we can pack up the rest of our belongings and arrange to have them shipped here. We'll also need to end the apartment lease and hire a cleaning service before we hand over the keys." Annie nodded her head in agreement. She knew there was so much that needed to be done but found herself avoiding everything. She was still reeling from everything that had transpired, over the past few weeks. Her bold statement insisting that she was moving to Murphy permanently and then, even worse, her rejection of Sam's marriage proposal.

"You're right," said Annie. She grabbed a notebook from the counter and began jotting down a to-do list. Sam rattled off a lengthy list of tasks that needed to be done, and Annie began to roll her eyes. *What am I, his secretary?* Her frustration began to get the best of her. To be successful, this trip was going to require a lot of planning and organization. She was stressing and needed to decompress and decided to take a short nap.

Annie awoke feeling much better. She added more items to the to-do-list, the apartment manager, the cleaning service, the moving company, and of course, their bosses and began to make arrangements one by one. *Oh my god, my boss won't see this coming!*

Annie had been a hybrid worker for a while now. She only went into the office a few days a week—working from home the remaining time. She jotted down her boss's name and made sure to underline it. She enjoyed working for the magazine. It was her first job after college, and she never felt the need to look elsewhere. Her boss was more than accommodating, especially once Molly joined her. She had developed a few intimate friendships along the way. She knew it would be Aleena she would miss the most. Although they were not close in age, they shared a sisterly bond that Annie knew could never be replaced.

Annie pushed herself away from the table with a heavy sigh. "Is this really happening?" she mumbled under her breath. Sam nodded his head yes. He was confused. He was hoping their trip back to New York would help to bring them some normalcy and give them both a chance to sort through some unresolved issues.

"Sam, I was thinking, what if instead of hiring a moving crew, we just moved ourselves back. We could rent a U-Haul and do it ourselves. I could see if my mom and dad would let Molly stay with them," Annie explained. She knew that Molly would be treated like a princess. Even though her mom was allergic to her, she couldn't resist falling in love with her. Annie noticed that most people, that met Molly, fell in love with her instantly.

Sam headed into town for supplies, and Annie hauled out the list of people and companies she needed to call. She didn't realize there was so much involved with the moving process. A quick phone call to her parents confirmed that Molly would be able to stay with them. Knowing that would make the trip just a little bit easier. Before Sam made it to the door, Annie shouted to him, "Sam, what days are we planning on going, and how long do you think we will be gone?" Sam thought it was comical that Annie was asking him for details about a trip that she had requested.

"I think we should plan to stay at the apartment from a Wednesday to a Sunday," Sam shouted! "I have some friends and coworkers that I want to see while we're there. Maybe we could plan a little dinner party." Annie thought about it for a few moments and agreed. Another phone call would need to be made to their favorite restaurant. Annie knew she had no plans to cook while they were in New York. Four days to wrap things up in New York and then a few days, on the road, back to Texas. Annie was looking forward to the little vacation. If everything went according to plan, they would be back home by that following Tuesday.

"May I go now?" Sam said with a chuckle. Annie waved her hand in the air with a big smile on her face.

I really do love Sam; maybe I just needed some more time?

CHAPTER 2

Planning the Trip Back to New York

Annie proceeded to call everyone on the list, including her mom. She was surprised when she called, and her dad answered, he rarely answered the phone unless her mother was not home.

"Hey, Dad," said Annie. "Sam and I are planning our trip back to New York. We need to pack up the rest of our belongings and say our final goodbyes. I thought it would be a good idea to rent a U-Haul and make the trip back ourselves. We really need some time to sort through everything that's been going on." Annie didn't wait for him to respond. "Can Molly stay with you while we are gone?" Annie could hear the excitement in her dad's voice, as he agreed without hesitation. She was glad he was the one who answered the phone.

"My little princess, at our house, while you're gone. I think we can do that," he chuckled. "I think even your mom will be on board with this one. She has become quite fond of Molly, — as long as she keeps her distance." They both laughed. Annie still thought most of her mom's allergies were in her head, but she couldn't tell her that. She smiled when she hung up the phone. At times like these she was happy to be living so close to her parents *I never realized how much I had missed them, until now.* It wasn't long ago she couldn't wait to move away from them.

Annie hung up the phone and sat for a moment. She reflected on her teenage years when living at home with her parents seemed impossible—when she looked forward to the day she would graduate and move far away. *Mom was overprotective and always in my business. If I said it was black, she would insist that it was white. Perhaps if she had been more understanding or at least met me in the middle, occasionally, maybe I never would have left Murphy in the first place.* Annie thought about how her life might have looked if she hadn't moved away. *A husband, a house with a white picket fence. I wonder If I would already have children. Do I even want children? How can I be in my late twenties and not know if I ever want to have children? Is this even normal?*

Annie's thoughts drifted to the relationship she had with her dad, while she was growing up. She wanted to cry when she thought about the years she has missed out on. *Oh Dad, you spoiled me rotten. Even if, sometimes, you had to hide it from mom. You always found a way to get me what I wanted. Well except for adopting any animals. That was a conversation that was never on the table. Everyone knew the answer was going to be no.*

Well, all this reminiscing isn't going to get my day started any sooner. Annie popped up from the chair and ran upstairs to take a shower. She knew Sam wouldn't be gone long. For some reason, she felt the need to look her best, even if that only meant a pair of jeans and a flannel shirt. Annie was no stranger to fashion. She had a way of making the simplest outfit look sexy. She laughed out loud, wondering how she had become that teenage girl again who was interested in dressing to impress.

She rummaged through her closet, realizing she needed to plan a big shopping trip while they were in New York. Jeans and sweatshirts were great, but Annie needed some sexy in her wardrobe as well. She needed to be herself—a little salty and a little sweet. She could always find what she wanted online, but there was just something special about New York City shopping. She gathered what she wanted to wear and headed to the bathroom— knowing that she had what she needed to get Sam's attention. Apparently, Molly thought Annie was taking too long. She barked at Annie, as if to say come on let's go. Annie let out an exaggerated sigh "You sure are my girl, Molly." The two were now inseparable, unless Sam was around— then she was all about her daddy.

Annie heard Sam calling to her just as she stepped out of the shower. "I'll be right down," she yelled. She pulled on her favorite jeans that hugged her in all the right places. Next came a purple and black button-down shirt. Annie opted to leave it half unbuttoned, to allow the tight-black camisole to peek through. Annie loved the way it hugged her breasts, making her boobs appear larger. Last came her signature high heels. a touch of makeup, some perfume, and yes, her favorite heart-shaped pendant necklace. Sam had bought it for her, years ago, on one of her birthdays. She secretly wondered if he would notice, or even better, if he would remember. One last look in the mirror.

"I must say Annie, you're looking pretty good!" Annie gave herself a full turn while admiring herself in the mirror.

She stopped for a quick second and was reminded of the days she and Sam lived in New York. Sam always noticed when she wanted him to. "You always dress to be noticed don't you Annie Jones?" Sam would say. *Well Sam, today I am doing this all for you—my best friend, who's heart I have broken. Now I am trying to win you back. I should not have given you my answer so quickly—without taking the time to think about what I really wanted.*

Annie made her way down the stairs. She heard Sam's voice and walked into the kitchen. When she saw the look on Sam's face, she couldn't help but smile.

"Annie Jones, you look absolutely amazing!" Sam's eyes locked onto the pendant. "I remember when I bought that for you." His smile faded as he continued to speak. "I was really happy then. I remember thinking that you and I..."

Annie could feel her heart racing, she wasn't prepared for what was coming. Before she could even regain her composure, there he was— standing within inches of her face—holding the pendant in his hand. His eyes looked sad. "I remember buying this for you a few years ago on your birthday. We were so happy, Annie." Sam dropped the pendant from his hand, and it made a thud sound on Annie's chest. *How can I feel so amazing one moment and then torn up inside the next?*

"We are still happy Sam. Things have just a changed a little. We have had a rough few months, but things will settle into place, I promise." Annie realized it was a mistake to say that when she saw the hurt in Sam's eyes followed by an abrupt outburst,

"Will it, Annie? Will things ever settle into place, and what exactly does that mean?" "Sam, we haven't been here very long. Why can't we just take things slow?" Annie knew Sam's feelings were hurt, but she wasn't the enemy.

Once again, Molly was the savior from uncomfortable moments. She was scratching at the door for someone to bring her outside. Annie was happy to oblige. She grabbed Molly and walked her out the door. Annie sat on the steps, avoiding Sam. She understood Sam's feeling of being rejected. *Should a girl marry someone just because they receive a proposal, should they?*

Annie loved Sam. She loved him like a brother or a friend. She didn't know. She didn't know that Sam was in love with her—they had never shared a romantic moment. They never so much as kissed. Her mind began to race as she sat there. *How could I have been this blind? Was he trying to tell me, and I just didn't pick up on it?* She knew Sam was angry, but when she thought hard about it, so was she. *How dare he!* Annie grabbed Molly and walked back into the house. Sam was no longer in the kitchen, and she didn't bother to look for him.

Sam decided to walk the property and think. He knew he was wrong for not sitting Annie down long ago and telling her how he truly felt. His fear of ruining his friendship with Annie has led him close to doing just that. *I should have told Annie a long time ago!* His mind raced back to the countless times he had told Annie he loved her. He also remembered that he never said that he was in love with her. So naturally she always understood it to be in a brotherly way and of course he never corrected it or pursued it. *I thought one day she would feel the same way about me.*

Sam wasn't in any hurry to return to the house, so he decided to take a walk toward the pond. It was his and Annie's favorite spot. He reached the pond and sat on the dock. The sun was hot, but the warm breeze made it tolerable. His thoughts quickly took him back to the first time Annie, Molly and he went swimming here. *I saw the look of desire in Annie eyes. I saw the way she looked me! I know now more than ever, it was more than a friendly look, it was desire, it was lust!* Sam wanted to rush back to the house and confront her, but he knew that was a terrible idea, instead he stripped out of his clothes and dove into the pond. The water felt refreshing as it splashed against his bare chest. *I am not giving up, Annie loves me! I just need her to see it!* Sam knew his entire future lay in the palm of Annie's hands. Sam's thoughts were interrupted when he heard Molly's bark. He swam over to the edge, pulling himself out of the water. He wasn't sure what had her so riled. He pulled his jeans on and threw his tee shirt over his shoulder as he headed back to the house.

CHAPTER 3

Annie's Mom Tries to Help

nnie heard a car pulling into the driveway. *Thank God!* She looked out the window to see her mom walking up the stairs. She was relieved to see her but not sure why her mom was here. That's just the way things are still done in Murphy, Texas — no reason needed for a visit. This would never happen in New York. No one, not even a neighbor, would ever stop by without at least a phone call first. Annie opened the door before her mom had a chance to knock. "Hi, Mom!" said Annie. Her voice was overly chipper,

"Oh no, Annie, what's the matter? I'm sorry, dear, but I can see right through that fake enthusiasm you're displaying right now."

Annie shrugged her shoulders and shook her head. She didn't want to discuss all the problems she was having right now. It occurred to her that she wasn't even sure where Sam was. "It's okay, Mom, nothing Sam and I can't work out."

Annie's mom didn't bother to respond as she made her

way to the kitchen with Molly in tow. Annie couldn't help but laugh as her mom began sneezing when Molly got close. "Annie, can you please take Molly upstairs, or put her in the playpen for a few moments?"

"Sure, Mom," said Annie. She lifted Molly in her arms, opened her playpen door, and nudged her in. Annie felt sad for her, Molly loved people, and she had no idea what an allergy was. Thankfully, Molly found a toy, that she'd left in there the other day, so she managed to keep herself entertained. Annie now wondered if her dad had even mentioned to her mom that Molly would be staying with them for a few days? And she was not sure that now was the time to find that out.

"What's up, Mom," asked Annie "You don't usually visit on the weekend, especially without Dad." *Oh my! Wait—is it the weekend? Time is moving so fast I've lost track.*

"Well, Annie, today is actually Tuesday, and I am here because I am worried about you and Sam," said Annie's frown-faced Mom. "I have done some thinking, and perhaps maybe you should have just accepted his proposal?" Annie was on fire! *Stay calm Annie, just stay calm.*

Annie tried her best to remain calm and not raise her voice. "Mom, I don't know who told you this, but they were out of line, and I don't think we should be having this conversation! This is between Sam and I. I am a grown woman now and can make grown decisions, especially ones that may impact the rest of my life!" Annie hoped that she wasn't too brash. She had been in town for barely a month, and already her mother was trying to control her. She could feel all the old anger and resentment coming back. She quickly remembered why she left Murphy years ago.

"I'm so sorry, Annie, you're right. I shouldn't go sticking

my nose in where it doesn't belong," said her mother. Annie wasn't sure if her mother was sincere, she was an expert at working the sympathy card. *That's not going to work this time, Mom. It hasn't for some time.* Just as Annie was about to respond, she heard Sam open the back door *O.K, he's back.*

Annie's mom stood up from the kitchen chair when she saw him "Hello Sam, you are looking refreshed. Did you go for a dip in the pond today," she asked? She had one of those bigger than life smiles on her face as watched Sam. He nodded as he walked over and gave her a hug. Annie watched the two of them embrace. She wasn't surprised by Rose's love for him. *Sam is family, he has been family for so many years now, he is like her son.* Sam walked to the counter and made himself another cup of coffee.

"Rose, can I get you a cup of coffee?"

Annie's mom nodded her head yes. "That would be wonderful." As Sam was carrying Rose's coffee to the table, he unknowingly blurted out, "Annie tells me that Molly will be staying with you and Ben while we take our trip back to New York." Annie nearly choked on her coffee, and she wasn't alone.

"Well, Sam," said Annie's mom. "I guess Ben forgot to mention this bit of information before I left the house." Annie held her breath, waiting for her mom to finish. She knew that even though her dad said Annie's mom would be delighted, it didn't really mean that she would be. "

"No need to worry, Sam, we will be happy to have Molly stay with us for a few days. After all, where else would she go?"

Annie exhaled a sigh of relief. She knew her options were limited with Molly.

"Please bring Molly's pen yard when you come. She will need a place to sleep," she added.

"What do the two you have planned for today?"

Annie waited for Sam to respond. After their conversation this morning, she wasn't sure they would be doing anything together. She just stood there smiling. *You sure are a clever one Mom. Sam may not know that your fishing, but I sure do. Now let's see if Sam bites.*

"Well, Rose, said Sam, we haven't figured that out yet, but if you and Ben would like to come over for dinner tonight, say around six, I could fix up something delicious."

Annie's mother didn't miss a beat. "Of course, we'll come dear. from what I have seen of your cooking, I know we won't disappointed! I do need to run. Ben and I will be here at six!"

Sam gave Rose a hug and peck on the cheek before Annie followed her to the door. She whispered in her mother's ear, "I saw what you were doing in there, Mom." Annie's mom gave her a puzzled look back, and Annie shook her head in disapproval. "It wasn't a question, Mom, it was a statement. We'll see you tonight."

Annie watched her mom walk down the stairs and get into her car. She wasn't sure where the years had gone. Her mom looked old today. Rose walked with a slight limp and seemed so much more fragile than she did years ago. Annie dismissed the thought from her mind. She had plenty going on and couldn't get caught up in that kind of thinking today.

Sam was busy preparing dinner for Annie's parents while she finished making the required phone calls — to ensure everything was set for their trip to New York. The plan was to take a flight into J.F.K. and grab a taxi to the U-Haul company, pack the rest of their belongings, and make the trip back.

"Sam, do you still want me to make the reservations for the dinner party on Saturday?" Annie stood silently, waiting for his response. At first Sam didn't respond, Annie wasn't sure if he was thinking about it or if he thought she was a fool for considering it.

"Sam?" Annie asked. Sam looked in Annie's direction, "Yes of course, dinner on Saturday." His response was unemotional, almost trance like.

The conversation was abruptly ended when Annie's mom–Rose and dad–Ben, arrived early for dinner.

CHAPTER 4

Dinner with the Parents

The three of them sat around the large table, on the back deck, as Sam bounced back and forth—keeping an eye on the evening meal. Molly found a good spot under the table, and Annie's mom didn't seem to mind her joining them. Annie's mom raved about what a great cook Sam was, and assured everyone that if she ate another bite, she would surely explode. Annie had to agree, Sam was a fantastic cook. This surprised her. When they were living in New York, they ate a lot of quick dinners or ordered out. Annie's dad chimed in." Sam, I'm an old man and have eaten a lot of prime rib in my time, but I have to say this is one of the best I have ever had!" Sam grinned from ear to ear in a proud but boyish way that Annie couldn't help but find adorable.

Annie and Sam were flying out early in the morning, so it was nice to just sit back and enjoy the quiet evening. Annie was thankful the conversation was light and enjoyable, and the evening was going as planned. Her mom helped clear the table and load the dishwasher. Sam and Ben sat outside discussing local history. Sam listened as Ben ran down the histories of the old farms, famous people who once lived in the area, and how much things have changed. Sam was most intrigued by the knowledge Ben had about the Sanctuary. Sam loved to hear Annie's dad talk about the previous owners, their children, grandchildren, and where they all were today. Ben looked at his watch and yelled to Annie's mom, who was still in the kitchen. "We should be going, Rose, and let these two get some sleep. They have a long, few days ahead of them." Annie nodded her head in agreement. She was already exhausted from the day and looking forward to snuggling up with Molly for the night. Annie and Sam said goodbye to her parents, and they both went upstairs to their separate bedrooms.

Annie pushed the door open to her bedroom. The room was large compared to her bedroom in New York. Under normal circumstances, this room had a relaxing happy feel to it. This was her happy place. A place to get away from it all, but tonight she felt differently. She laid sprawled out on the bed, staring at the ceiling. The tension between her and Sam was taking its toll. Annie's mind replayed the events that led the two of them to where they are today, and she wished she could turn back time. There was a part of her that wished her Uncle Jack had never died and certainly never left her this Sanctuary. Then she realized she wouldn't have Molly if none of that had happened. Annie felt the tears escaping from her eyes. Luckily, Molly had joined her, in her room, she pulled Molly up to her chest and laid there staring at the ceiling. The silence from outside was deafening. As she lay there, in the darkness, she realized that she missed the New York lights and night noise. Annie thought she heard a noise coming from Sam's room. She held her breath so she could hear. *Is that Sam?*

Sam stood in his bedroom looking out of the window. It was too early for him to go to bed but when Annie's parents had left for the evening, he had followed Annie and Molly upstairs. He stood there looking out into the darkness. The sky was dark, and Sam could see the stars. There was silence outside, not even the peepers were singing tonight. He sat on the bed, slowly removing his shoes— one by one. he thought about all the events that got him here. It was his love for Annie that got him here. He would follow her to the moon if she asked. Sam scolded himself for being behaving so foolishly. *I have a lot going for me. I have a great job, make a decent wage, I am good looking. Heck I even work out at the gym every day. How many men my age still does that? Any woman should be happy to call me their husband including Annie Jones! Who does she think she is— playing with me like this!* Sam grabbed the first thing he could find on the end stand, his cellphone, and without hesitation or thought, he hurled it across the room. He watched in slow motion, as it swirled through the air. He was instantly embarrassed by what he had just done. *Jesus Sam, really, not the eight-hundred-dollar phone! He* jumped off the bed and ran over to where the phone had landed., He was certain he would be looking for a place to buy a new phone in the morning. Much to his surprise, the phone remained intact. *That phone case I purchased was worth every penny.* Sam heard a knock on his door.

"Sam are you okay?" Annie was just outside the door. She must have heard the noise when the phone hit the floor.

"I'm fine Annie, go back to bed." Sam didn't bother to open the door and Annie didn't pursue it any further.

CHAPTER 5

The Day of the Flight

Annie woke to the sound of her phone buzzing. She wasn't sure where the night had gone, but she knew she wasn't ready to start her day yet. She grabbed her phone and quickly hit the snooze. It was too late; Molly wasn't having any of it. She was already prancing around—looking to start her day. "Molly, come back up on the bed and lay down with me. We still have a few minutes." Annie's voice went unnoticed, Molly continued to pace back and forth. "Oh, fine!" said Annie. "We can get up. I guess you are ready to start your day, huh, little girl?" Annie patted Molly on the head as she opened the door.

Annie could hear the water running, in the bathroom—Sam was taking a shower. He was usually the first to rise, even in New York. Sometimes he was out the door before Annie crawled out of bed. Even so, Annie noticed that he was sleeping even less these days.

Sam had spent most of the past few days trying to figure out how to make things work and worrying what might become of him. He didn't own the house. He had no rights to any of it. He couldn't help but wonder where that would leave him, down the road. He wondered what would happen if Annie started dating someone. All these thoughts contributed to his sleepless nights. He was struggling with finding the solutions.

Molly ran down the stairs and was waiting by her food dish. Annie turned the Keurig on and proceeded to feed the little Diva. She was sure Molly had lost a few pounds since being here, but she wasn't sure how. She certainly ate the same gourmet food and plenty of it. "Okay, little girl, you finish eating while I go pack up your playpen." Annie could not help but chuckle to herself. Thinking of Molly's play yard as a playpen brought an image to her mind of a little baby, not a dog.

A few moments later, Sam came running down the stairs as if he were on fire. "Annie, do you have everything packed and ready to go?" Annie smiled in Sam's direction and commented to Molly loud enough for him to hear. "Tell daddy we are all packed up and ready to go!" Sam laughed as he grabbed the bags by the door and made his way to the car.

Sam was loading the car while Annie took one last look around the house to make sure everything was turned off and the back door was locked. She had asked her brother, Brian, to stop in and check on things, while they were gone. Annie was headed for the door when she heard Sam yelling, "Annie, we're going to miss the flight, if you don't hurry!" She grabbed Molly and rushed out the door, turning the knob to be sure it was locked. *You can never be too safe.* Like the perfect little family, they loaded into the truck. It was a short drive to Annie's parent's house, and the temperature was already beginning to rise. Mornings in Texas can heat up quickly.

Luckily, the weather will be a bit cooler when they arrive in New York. Something occurred to Annie as she watched Sam approach. Sam very seldom wore shorts in public, even with temperatures as warm as they have been. Today would be no exception, she smiled at him as he walked closer, dressed in his usual Texan attire.

Annie was with him when he picked up a few tee shirts and jeans at one of the downtown stores. She loved that since living in Texas, he wore only fitted tee shirts which hugged his abs and his sculpted shoulders, Sam worked out religiously and it showed. She enjoyed being able to enjoy the fruits of his labor. They had grabbed a few pairs of Levi jeans to finish the look. Annie scanned him from head to toe. She admired the cowboy boots that she'd helped him pick out just a week ago. *Yep, he was beginning to look like a true Texan, and boy, was he easy on the eyes, especially today.*

Sam looked relaxed as Annie watched him hand over the playpen to Annie's dad. She wasn't sure how he could appear so relaxed when just moments before, he had been shouting to her that they were going to miss their flight. *Sam was a little dramatic at times especially if it involved being late.*

They reached the airport in plenty of time. Sam stood looking out the window of the airport, gazing up at the sky. Annie wasn't sure what he was thinking, but she was sure she wasn't about to ask. She knew things had been tense between them. His feelings were still hurt, and his ego was still wounded from Annie's proposal rejection. *We are going to get through this, Sam is my best friend and I love him. They say time heals all wounds; I guess we'll find out if that's true.*

She sat quietly next to him, pretending to read a book on her kindle, but her mind was all over the place, and it was impossible to do any reading. Annie sat her kindle down when she heard a woman's voice. She recognized the voice and fake giggle right away. The woman had already sat down on the other side of Sam and was touching his arm as she spoke. *You must be kidding me! Kristina, the pet transport servicewoman She assisted in Molly's transport from New York to Texas. What in the world is she doing here, and why is she always touching on Sam? She couldn't keep her hands off him then, and apparently, she is having the same problem today!*

Annie's blood was boiling. She tried to remain calm as Sam reintroduced the two of them. Annie gave her a quick nod and looked down, pretending to read—trying to keep her composure. She didn't understand why she was so annoyed with this young woman, but Kristina triggered every jealousy button Annie had, and then some. Annie was even more sickened by Sam and his eagerness to participate in the outrageous, teenage flirting! Annie excused herself, although she wasn't sure why she bothered to say anything at all. The two of them were oblivious to anything, or anyone around them. Annie wandered around the airport until she found the restroom. She rushed into the stall. Her heart was racing, and she was convinced she might be having a panic attack — although she had never had one before. *Get ahold of yourself. Sam is your roommate—not your boyfriend or even fiancé. He could have been yours it could have been you that he was flirting with. It was ME that he asked to marry him only weeks ago. Has he forgotten that? How can he move so quickly without any acknowledgment of how I might feel? Maybe I should have accepted his proposal and none of this would be happening right now!*

Annie exited the restroom, feeling a bit more composed as she headed back. She was disappointed at the outfit she chose. *Maybe I should have gone with those tight-fitting jeans, fitted blouse and heels.*

Sam was a huge fan of that look, but it seemed like a ridiculous idea this morning. Annie looked at the time on her phone. Another thirty minutes or so, and they would be able to board the plane. *Please, please tell me Kristina is not flying to New York with us.* Annie was relieved when she got back to her seat, Kristina was gone. Annie didn't ask where she went or if she would be coming back. She didn't want to know; she was hoping that someone would come and sit next to Sam — just in case Kristina planned to come back.

"Annie, I was getting worried, they announced that we would be boarding the plane soon, and you weren't back yet."

Stay calm and use your friendly voice. Annie knew that she tended to fly off the handle and would need some time to calm down once she did. She wasn't going to let that happen here. She made eye contact with Sam and said," I'm sorry Sam there was a long line." Sam nodded his head and went back to gazing at the sky. Thankfully, a few moments later, Annie heard the flight attendant, on the loudspeaker announcing their plane's boarding. "It's about time," Annie blurted out! She had become increasingly anxious sitting there with Sam— in complete silence. She hoped the trip was going to get better: soon. Sam and Annie boarded the plane.

It was a small plane in comparison to the one they had taken from New York to Texas a short time ago. Annie didn't mind besides, in just a short three and a half hours they would arrive at the J.F.K. airport. A quick cab ride would bring them to the U-Haul company, where their truck would be waiting to be picked up. The plan was to get it to the apartment building, load it up with their belongings and head out on Sunday morning, for the drive back to Texas. Annie realized now how little thought she had put into the return trip back home, certainly not as much thought as getting to New York.

Sam took hold of Annie's hand as they scurried to the baggage claim area. Annie had somehow forgotten how overwhelmingly busy the J.F.K airport could be. It was times like this that Annie was thankful that Sam was a take-charge kind of person. He was smart, quick on his feet and had a calming demeanor—everything that they needed for situations like this. He would often tell Annie, "If you dawdle, you are going to lose your spot, in line and in life." Annie smiled at the thought. *So much truth in such a short statement.*

Sam moved Annie quickly through the airport and called to the first cab he saw. The cab driver pulled up, and Sam loaded their bags. The conversation was light as the driver made his way to the U-Haul company. Annie wandered around the parking lot, checking out the different sized U-hauls. She never thought to ask Sam if he had driven a large truck. After what seemed like an eternity, Sam came out with the keys... She watched him as he skipped toward her. There it was again, that boyish charm that she absolutely adored. Annie laughed as he approached her. "This is going to be an adventure. I've never had the opportunity of driving a U-Haul in New York. I hope you brought darkened sunglasses with you. This is something you may not want to see," he laughed.

Annie never thought about the crazy New York traffic or the narrow city streets. Her planning for a U-Haul went as far as reserving one and stopped there. She remembered being surprised at how easily Sam had accepted her suggestion to rent a U-Haul and drive themselves back. She just assumed he had done it before. She now wondered if he had given any thought to it or if he just said yes because it was Annie doing the asking? *Well, here we are, and this is happening.*

CHAPTER 6

Annie Meets Chet

Annie didn't recognize the route Sam was taking. *Maybe he knows his way around the outskirts of the city? Sam always was full of surprises.* Annie let the tension fall away from her shoulders, relaxing herself back into her seat. She marveled at the homes they passed while driving through the little neighborhoods. They were all small, quaint, and perfect. Annie was sure that they were out of her price range. The taxes alone were probably more than her annual salary. She checked the GPS and told Sam, "We're about five minutes away, according to this." Sam shook his head, in acknowledgement, and smiled. He knew this route very well, and he knew exactly where they were and how long it would take to get there. He took this route, knowing what a nice drive it would be. It would be a good opportunity for them both to relax. He drove for a few more blocks before turning into a narrow driveway. There was just enough room on either side of the truck for them to squeeze out. Sam stepped out of the van;

Annie followed. A white-haired man, with a warm smile, approached them.

"Annie, this is my good friend, Chet. He and I go way back. Chet was a client of mine a few years back. His company hired ours to take the lead in one of their engineering projects. Long story short, I wined and dined him, made his company lots of money and we have been friends ever since."

Chet chimed in, "Yeah those were some great dinners we had, more booze than food. I miss those dinner meetings, but to be quite honest, retired life is even better than I imagined." Annie smiled. She could tell by Chet's relaxed demeanor; retired life agreed with him.

"Chet has offered to drive us back to the apartment," explained Sam.

Annie reached out and shook his hand, trying to get a read on his age. *No age spots or any other telltale signs of senior citizen status. He is not as old as his white hair would have you believe.* Chet reached for Annie's hand, and gently brought it to his lips and kissed it. *How charming.* Annie felt the shakiness of his hand as he moved her hand to his lips. She found it odd since other than his white hair, he appeared young. "It's my pleasure to finally meet you, Annie. I have heard so much about you over the years. Having never met you, I was beginning to think Sam had an imaginary girlfriend?"

Annie's eyes grew wide, she looked directly at Sam with a puzzled look. She wondered what Sam had been telling Chet all these years. She gathered from Chet's comments that he and Sam communicated on a fairly regular basis. *How is that I haven't heard more about this man. Does Sam have secrets?* Annie just smiled, she wouldn't even know where to begin a conversation as big as that one, but she knew that she would be discussing it with Sam at another time.

Chet walked over to his garage, pulling on the rope that hung from the ceiling—the door opened. "This is my baby and today you both get the honor of riding in it." Chet beamed with pride. Sam seemed unphased by the beautiful car. Annie could only guess that he had seen it before. She moved forward to get a closer look.

"Come on Annie, can you guess the make and model?" Chet teased.

"I don't know much about cars but it's definitely a Mustang!" Chet smiled. "You're right! This baby is a nineteen sixty-six Mustang!"

"Chet this Mustang is gorgeous! Have you done the work yourself," asked Annie? She climbed into the back seat—the interior had all been meticulous refinished. She settled back into the seat and listened to the two men banter back and forth. Annie could tell Sam was fond of Chet, she was surprised she hadn't heard more about him. She wasn't sure when she would bring up Sam's comment about her being his girlfriend, but she knew it wasn't going to be anytime soon. He was still licking his wounds, so she was going to leave it alone: for now.

When they arrived at the apartment, Chet pulled over and let them off at the curb. They knew all too well that finding a parking spot even remotely close to the building would be impossible. Sam grabbed their bags from the curb and headed for the entrance—Annie followed closely.

Annie could smell the aroma from several area restaurants. She had missed those smells and only now realized how much. Sam continued to lead the way—he moved at a fast pace. Annie didn't seem to mind much. It allowed her to think about all the loose ends that needed to be tied up, before heading back to Murphy.

Sam pulled the keys from his pocket and unlocked the door.

"After you, my lady," he said. They smiled at each other, and Annie held out her hand to be kissed. Sam obliged and the two laughed as they entered the apartment.

Annie walked through the door and was, almost immediately, flooded with emotion. It was like taking a step back in time before anything had ever happened. The move to Texas had taken its toll on both of them. This apartment represented a time when they were happy living as roommates—when there was no attraction between the two of them. Annie wondered if she might have been wrong about that.

Annie sat her bags down and walked to the front of the living room. The sheer curtains were still on the windows, and Annie decided she should leave them as they are. She wouldn't have any use for them anymore. Annie pulled the curtain away and looked out the window. *Ah, her favorite spot. How often I had gazed out this window watching the hustle and bustle — wondering where people were headed. Did they have families, jobs?*

Annie's thoughts were interrupted by Sam moving things around the kitchen. She turned around to see what he was doing and paused. Sam didn't resemble the guy she had lived with for so many years in this apartment. He was so much more now. It was almost impossible for her to look at him without feeling an underlying sexual current raging through her. She had no control over these feelings. It would be wrong for her to tell him how she felt. It would confuse him and encourage him to mention the marriage proposal again. Annie knew she had to keep these feelings to herself, at least for now. *I just want to enjoy the few days we have here in New York.*

Sam caught Annie staring at him. He didn't say a word

but just smiled. Annie quickly turned looking the other way. *Sam you really are the package deal! You are incredibly handsome, you are kind, generous!* Annie scanned the living room. It somehow seemed much emptier than it did before they left. The furniture was sparse, and for that, she was thankful. *We should be able to get most of this ourselves.*

CHAPTER 7

Sam Lashes Out!

Annie's thoughts were interrupted by a knock at the door. She followed Sam as he walked toward the door. She thought it was odd that someone would be visiting them—they just arrived. Annie peeked around Sam and saw the apartment manager. Joe was a young man in his thirties. Annie was confident even she was taller than he was, which would put him around 5 foot. He was as big around as he was tall. His jet-black hair was pulled back in a ponytail, and he sported a handlebar mustache. He was always in uniform, making it impossible for Annie to guess what style of clothes he would wear.

"Hey, Joe," said Sam. "I was expecting you to come by—just not so soon."

"Well, Sam, your apartment just happens to be in high demand. We have already had several prospective tenants reach out, and they are all eager to take a tour. Some are from other neighborhoods looking to get closer to downtown, and others already live in the building and are just looking for an upgrade."

Annie immediately felt sick to her stomach. Until now she was excited, her thoughts had been centered around packing up and moving. She was about to start a new chapter in her life. A new adventure was about to unfold for her. However, the idea of this apartment being rented to someone else and no longer belonging to them made her feel ill. This had been their home for years, and it's not like they were moving because they didn't like the place. Joe pushed the papers in front of Sam's face and made his way into the apartment. Annie had never seen Joe act so aggressively. Joe was probably under pressure to get the apartment flipped to the next tenant. *Money, the root of all evil, and apparently rude behavior.*

"Sam, can we talk," asked Annie?

"What's up, Annie? This is what you wanted, isn't it," he asked?

Annie paused, she didn't know how to respond without coming across childishly. She wanted to live in their new home, in Texas, but didn't want to give up their home in New York. She knew she was being ridiculous.

Sam agreed, "Annie, you're insane! You make all these decisions and then want to change everything at the last minute. Annie Jones, I am sick and tired of being in your hamster on a wheel! You are selfish and only care about yourself! It was a mistake for me to give up my life for you!" You will never know what you want!"

Sam stormed out the door—slamming it behind him.

Annie could feel the tears welling up into her eyes. Sam's response was so out of character. Joe stood there for a minute, looking for an easy escape. Annie sulked her way into her bedroom and laid on the queen size bed. *I miss this room, I miss this bed.* She had a flashback, to the day they visited the furniture store to pick out her bedroom set. He teased her when she told him she wanted a queen-size bed. Annie laughed when she recalled the memory. *"Annie Jones, I have a double bed, and that's plenty of room for me! Oh no, don't tell me, you have a secret wish to have wild parties and entertain young men, then when they're too tired to go home, you'll have plenty of room in your bed for your guests to stay over!"*

She laid on her back, staring at the ceiling. She could hear the noise outside. She was sure she heard music playing in the distance. Frustrated by all the noise, she rolled over on her side, and then she saw it: her favorite picture. She and Sam were happy then.

Annie could feel the tears streaming down her cheeks. It wasn't just this memory. There were so many more amazing memories that they shared together. Things were simpler when there was no confusion about the relationship. They were Sam and Annie, buddies, best friends, and roommates. Now, it seemed so long ago and far away. It seemed like Sam couldn't talk to her, anymore, without getting upset. He was hurt, and she was constantly walking on eggshells. *They just needed time to figure it out.*

Annie heard a noise, and she listened. She was confident she had locked the door before marching into her bedroom, but now she wasn't sure. Within seconds, she knew it was Sam. He stomped his feet, as he walked, the way a child would.

Annie braced herself as she rolled from the bed. She knew they needed to talk, and the sooner, the better. She opened her bedroom door quietly and paused. At that very second, she realized Molly wasn't at her feet, and she wanted to cry.

She wished Molly was there with her for moral support. The very thought of Molly brought tears to her eyes. The stress of the trip has taken its toll. She felt empty inside and alone. *Get ahold of yourself, Annie. This conversation needs to be had, and it needs to be done: now.*

Sam saw Annie coming from her room and started walking toward her. Before she could say mutter a word, Sam swooped her up in his arms and held her. Annie could feel the heat from his body and his breath on the nape of her neck. Annie couldn't control her emotions any longer. She buried her face into his chest and stood there sobbing. She was sure this hug was going down in history as the longest hug ever. Annie could feel his lungs filling up with air as he squeezed her tighter and his subtle breath when he let the air out. The smell of his cologne tingled in her nose as she buried herself even farther into his chest. She could feel the sexual tension rising, and it scared her. She pulled away. Sam took her by the shoulders and said, "Annie, I want you to know I am so sorry. I am sorry for my outbursts. I am sorry for not listening to you, and most of all, I am sorry that I love you more than life itself!"

Annie was speechless. How do I begin to respond to any of those statements? And why did Sam have to ruin the moment by talking?

Annie nodded, in agreement to avoid that ugly trip down the rabbit hole.

"Sam, can we please talk about all of this later? Let's go grab a bite to eat and wander the shops." Sam agreed even though Annie knew he wasn't a fan of shopping, he always would tag along just for the company.

Phew. I just want one day where things can feel normal, the way we used to be: happy. The phone rang, and it startled Annie. She glanced down at her phone. It was her mom. She would hold her breath when she saw her parents' number, afraid something might be wrong. "Hi Mom, is everything okay?"

Annie's mom responded in a rather cheerful voice, "Oh yes Annie, we are taking Molly to the dog park today. She is such a joy to have around."

I wanted to call before we left in case you tried to reach us." Annie smiled. "Thank you, Mom, for everything. Molly is lucky to have a grandma like you. Sam heard the conversation and smiled when Annie ended the call.

"Molly is one lucky pup!"

—◆—

CHAPTER 8

A Tall Favor to Ask

S am made sure to lock the apartment door as he and Annie made their way to the elevator. Annie didn't recognize the tall, black-haired man, who smiled at them. "Annie, this is Kevin," said Sam.

"Kevin and I went to college together before I transferred to NYU.

Kevin reached for Annie's hand, "Hey Annie, it's a pleasure to finally meet you." Annie smiled, "it's nice to meet you, Kevin. I had no idea that one of Sam's old college buddies lived here,"

"I'm sorry Annie, we've been so busy lately, I forgot to mention it to you. Kevin moved in while you were at your uncle's funeral," Sam explained. *How do you forget to tell me that?*

Annie couldn't help but stare at Kevin. He was attractive enough but in a soccer dad kind of way. He was at least six-foot tall with thinning black hair. His brown eyes were big and round, giving him a look of kindness. Annie noticed a silver band, snuggly placed on his left ring finger. She was sure it had been on his finger for a while. His finger looked as though it was growing around the band. For some reason this made her smile. Annie's mind drifted away as the two of them chattered on about sports and their old college days.

As they were stepping from the elevator, Sam invited Kevin to join them for lunch. Deep-down, Annie was praying he would say no, but the Universe doesn't always listen, and within seconds, Kevin agreed. "Sure, man," Kevin said excitedly. "My wife Kate is working late, and I was about to grab a bite to eat myself."

Sam mentioned a new Pub that opened not too long ago and was a short jaunt from the apartment. Annie followed behind like a child as the two men chatted on and on about "the good old days."

When they finally reached the Pub, Sam stepped out the way and opened the door for her, ushering her inside. "Good choice," said Annie. She turned her head to look at Sam.

. The inside was much more spacious than it appeared to be from the outside. A mahogany bar, lined with matching stools ran the length of the room. A few high tables sat nestled in front of the windows, while the rest of the area was set up with customary dining tables. The knotty-pine walls were covered with pictures. Annie couldn't help but notice an image of the twin towers before the 911. Most of the wall images were of New Yorkers being New Yorkers. Someone with an excellent eye shot these photos. Annie was intrigued. She strolled away from the men momentarily as her eyes scoured the images. She spotted a picture of a young woman squatting down, handing a child an ice cream cone. The photo captured the essence of that moment perfectly. A picture of a young boy holding his bike against a building, while pondering what to do about his flat-tired bike, seemed to draw Annie's attention. Annie was mesmerized by all the pictures and knew she had to find out who the photographer was.

Sam and Kevin were already seated and had ordered drinks. Sam chose to sit at the high table rather than the bar, and Annie was content with his choice. "The table by the window," she had heard Sam say. It was the perfect spot.

Annie looked out the window while the two men continued their chatter.

And they say women love to talk.

Annie found the afternoon enjoyable. The sun was shining, and since her favorite pastime was people watching, she was in the right spot.

Annie hadn't really been paying any attention to their conversations until she heard Kevin say the words, "Hey man, I need a favor!"

Annie's ears perked up, and she caught herself leaning in a little closer, making sure she heard him correctly. Apparently, Sam was caught off guard as well. "Excuse me?" Annie heard Sam say. Kevin looked down and fidgeted with his watch.

"Do you remember my sister, Julee? Well, she has been battling cancer for the past year, she is having surgery on Thursday. She asked that Kate and I look after her dog Jersey until she was released. Sam, I know it's an unreasonable ask, but I have listened to you go on and on about Molly, and I know you planned to stay here at least until Sunday. You see, Kate and I, we don't really get along with dogs, you know, we're just not dog people. I promise Sam, it's only until Sunday."

Sam made a half –hearted attempt to tell Kevin why they couldn't do it —stuttering all the way through. Then without any thought, Annie blurted out, "We can take him, Kevin, we are going to be here anyway, and I would love the company! My heart has been missing our little girl Molly anyway, and it's just for a few days, right?"

Annie grinned when she saw the reaction on Sam's face. "Annie, are you sure this is a good idea? I mean, we're supposed to be packing up our stuff and leaving?" Annie assured Sam that, without a doubt, it was the right thing to do. She would want someone to do the same for her if she were in his sister's shoes. She secretly hoped that it might take them a little longer to get packed up—now that they would be attending to Jersey. She had forgotten how much she missed New York.

Sam handed Kevin a piece of paper with his phone number on it, telling him to bring Jersey to their apartment anytime this evening, or tomorrow. Kevin shook Sam's hand. "Thank you so much for helping out my family like this man. I owe you one." Sam nodded.

They paid the tab, and Annie asked the waiter about the photographer. She was informed that he was a local guy who just happened to be doing the bar owner a favor. Albert, the bars owner, and he are good friends. Matt, the photographer wanted a place to display his work and Albert wanted some wall art. It was a win for them both.

"If you'll wait for one-moment, ma'am, I can get his number for you. He is a good friend of Alberts, the bar owner, and he visits quite often. The guy's name is Matthew Stevens, and he left his number with me in case Albert was looking for more photos. He lost his wife and their only daughter, Lizzy, in a terrible car accident. At the time, he had been a successful stockbroker but gave it all up after her death. Anyway, I'll go and grab his number for you." said the waiter.

The young man returned a few moments later and handed Annie the paper with the number on it. Annie thanked the young man as she shoved the paper into her purse. As they headed out the front door, Kevin mentioned he was going to head off in the other direction. He had some errands to finish up and would be in touch soon. He thanked them once again as they said their goodbyes, and off they went in different directions.

As they strolled toward the apartment they talked about Kevin, Kevin's sister Julee, her cancer, and their new responsibility. They joined arms as they walked along the street. Everything seemed so alive and vibrant. They passed all the little shops that Annie had visited so frequently. They walk past the jewelry store where she had purchased the necklace for her mom before trip back home that changed their life forever. That's when it hit her... Annie realized that things had changed forever. She tried to push the thought from her mind. They were in New York, the mood was light, and she was determined to enjoy every minute...

From a distance, they heard live music playing. "Come on, Sam, let's go check it out!" He rolled his eyes. Sam was sure the music he was hearing wasn't his kind of music, but he agreed. They had no place to be, and it felt good to be getting along. *This is just the opportunity we need, a chance to blow off some steam, relax and reconnect.* Annie laughed while pulling on his arm. "This will be fun Sam!"

As it turned out, the live music was coming from the small park near the apartment. Sam found them a bench to sit on, near the stage. They sat there listening to the music. They both agreed that it was some form of soul and R&B mix. The band had some talent. At the end of the show, Sam walked over and threw a twenty-dollar bill in the donation hat. he returned to Annie, who was still sitting on the bench and held out his hand. Annie could feel the heat rising inside of her. It was like electricity that made its way through every cell of her body. She wanted to smile or say something, but for some reason she couldn't. She just held out her hand and allowed him to pull her to her feet. His eyes were mesmerizing. She was sure at this moment, he was seeing into her soul. They walked back to the apartment hand in hand. Annie was on cloud nine, and she was confident Sam felt the same way.

They had just about reached the apartment building, and Annie heard Sam's phone ring. He stepped off to the side and answered the phone. He motioned for Annie to come closer. "It's Kevin on the phone. He wants to bring Jersey now." Annie was surprised. She thought they had at least until this evening.

"Yes, of course, she said. Ask him if we need anything, dog food, treats?" Annie heard Sam ask the questions. She knew the answers by watching him shake his head no. Sam hung up the phone as they rushed to get back to the apartment. He unlocked the door and scooted Annie into the apartment. She loved it when Sam took charge. It gave her a sense of security.

Annie thought it was comical that the two of them scurried around the apartment picking up anything that a Puggle might find interesting enough to chew, eat, or destroy. *I know what Molly's temptations are, but I have no idea what Jersey's might be? I wonder why the name Jersey? Well, I can only guess that Kevin's sister lives in Jersey or perhaps did at one time. Of course, that's only my assumption. Why else would someone name their pup Jersey? I wonder if his sister had Jersey since he was a pup? We don't know much about Jersey at all. How old is he? Does he like cats? Annie laughed out loud. Why do I care if he likes cats? I don't have any cats!*

Sam tapped Annie on the shoulders, and she let out a scream. "I guess you were deep in thought, huh, Annie?"

Before Annie could answer, there was a knock at the door. Annie and Sam both stood silently holding their breath, for what, Annie wasn't sure. After a few moments, Sam walked over and opened the door. There they were, Kevin and Jersey.

CHAPTER 9

Jersey's Arrival

Annie's eyes grew wide. She was expecting to see a Puggle the size of Molly. She had no idea that Puggle's shapes and sizes could vary so much... Jersey was not a petite Puggle— to say the least. He was much taller than Molly and very muscular. Annie could make out the defining lines of muscles he had on his shoulders and hind legs. Even his paws were twice the size of Molly's. *he looks like the Arnold Schwarzenegger of puggles.* Annie moved her eyes to Jersey's face and saw the biggest smile. Her heart melted. She stared into Jersey's big brown eyes, trying to capture the essence of his soul. *Oh, you're just a gentle giant.*

Annie quickly wiped away a tear before Kevin or Sam had a chance to notice. She felt sadness for Jersey. She didn't know how long Kevin's sister had been in and out of the hospital. Annie was sure that Jersey missed her and was confused. She could tell that Jersey was deeply loved and cared for. He came with a little ditty bag of his own. Annie didn't bother to open it at that time, but she did notice that Jersey wore a similar sweater to what she had purchased for Molly awhile back. She could see, from the tag, that it came from the same store. *It was obvious they had no problem spending money on him.*

Sam opened the door wider, allowing for their new guests to enter the apartment. Kevin handed the leash to Annie. and she removed it. It was a sturdy leash. Annie could only imagine the strength Jersey would have if something were to catch his eye. *Yeah, this little he-man probably needs a good strong leash.*

"Annie, I know you are used to having Molly around, but you should know a few things about Jersey. He is stubborn at times, and he can be a little sassy," Kevin explained. Annie laughed; she knew all too well about sassy Puggles. She learned that rather quickly about Molly as well.

Kevin continued with what Annie considered to be unnecessary information. "His favorite place to sleep during the day is on his bed. I'll bring that over a little later. However, at nighttime, he's used to sleeping with my sister, so if you wouldn't mind? I am sure he's going to be out of sorts. He has been moved from home to home recently, and I am sure it will take him some time to feel comfortable."

Annie made a point to ask Kevin again, "This is only until Sunday, right Kevin?"

Kevin hesitated, "Yes, yes, of course, only until Sunday."

"That won't be a problem," said Annie. She was sizing up Jersey, secretly wondering just how much of her bed would be left for her. She smiled at the thought.

Annie watched as Kevin made his way to the door without stopping to say anything to Jersey. She scowled as he walked away and couldn't help but ask, "Aren't you at least going to say goodbye to Jersey?" Kevin turned around abruptly to see

Annie who was squatted down next to Jersey, giving him the death stare. Annie couldn't help but be angry. *Who walks away from a dog without even a goodbye?* He walked back over and patted Jersey on the head as he looked for Annie's approval. *It was the very least he could do.*

Sam walked Kevin to the door, they shook hands and Sam closed it behind him. He made his way into the kitchen. Annie could hear him shuffling through the cupboards. She wasn't sure what he expected to find, but she could tell by the amount of time it was taking him—he wasn't finding what he was looking for.

"Annie, are you hungry?" She didn't bother to get up from the floor, where she and Jersey were getting to know one another.

Suddenly, something caught Jersey's eye and he stood up. She wasn't sure where he was off to, but he was doing so quickly. Jersey darted across the room to Molly's toybox—a wicker basket filled with toys. *What did you find Jersey?* She smiled as she watched him bury his nose, into the basket, until he found what he wanted.

Annie laughed hysterically when she saw what he had chosen. It was the Lamb Chop doll—one of Molly's favorites toys. Annie was sure that if Molly were there, she would not be happy about this. Annie ran to grab her phone, from the coffee table—this picture was going to be a keeper. She would be sharing it with his momma for sure.

Annie sat on the floor, waiting to see if Jersey would return. Despite his size and masculine look, he looked adorable carrying around Molly's Lamb chop doll. Annie watched to see what his intentions were. *I hope he doesn't plan to destroy Lamb Chop. Molly would never forgive him or me for, allowing him to have it.*

"Annie!" Sam called out again, "Are you hungry?" She wasn't hungry but she could tell he was. After all, they were in New York where the choices were many, and delivery was an option. *Who could say no?*

"Sure, Sam, go ahead and order some delivery—your choice. I want to give Jersey a chance to settle in." Annie could always tell when Sam was stress eating, *I hope he doesn't get fat from all this eating.*

"Pizza it is!" shouted Sam. He dialed and ordered. He was excited to have Grub Hub. Annie liked the way Sam was able to find joy in the little everyday things. When the pizza arrived, Sam grabbed a few pieces for him and Annie and delivered it to the living room— where Annie and Jersey sat waiting. Jersey drooled as he stared at the pizza. "You wouldn't know you had just eaten an hour ago. You boys sure do love your pizza!" Annie smiles as she tears off a piece and hands it to him. Jersey gobbles up the first piece and guilts her into another.

"Okay Jersey, that's it." Jersey had drool escaping from his mouth—he seemed to be mesmerized. His glazed-over eyes followed the slice of pizza as though his life depended on him having a bite of it—immediately. Annie couldn't help but laugh and point out the obvious to Sam. "Aww, Jersey, my guess is you really love pizza, don't you, boy?"

Annie didn't waste any time tearing apart the slice to share with her new buddy. She was surprised at how quickly he devoured it, as though he was starving But, she knew the truth, he had his dinner only an hour ago. Annie reached out to pet Jersey. "You are such a hungry little fella, I'll go and grab us one more piece, but that's going to be all for tonight. It's getting late, and we still must do the dreaded late-night pee-walk." This was the one thing Annie didn't miss, the trip down the elevator, out the door, and slipping around back just for just a five-second pee.

Annie gathered the plates and headed towards the kitchen to clean up. She heard a funny howl coming from the other room. She looked back and saw Jersey standing at the door waiting for someone to notice. Annie knew right away that he was asking to go out. She grabbed a towel, to dry her hands and headed towards Jersey. Before she could get to the door, Sam had the leash in his hand and was walking toward Jersey.

"I'll take him out, Annie. Jersey, and I can share some guy-talk while you finish up in here." Annie smiled and blew Sam a kiss.

"Thanks, Sam!" "You be a good boy Jersey, and I'll see you in a few." *Sam really is terrific!*

Annie was sitting in the living room when the two of them came back. She told Sam that she was going to her bedroom to give her mom a call. It was a little after nine Annie missed Molly, and she wanted to call before it got too late This was the first time, she had been away from her in a while, and she felt a need to reconnect. "Jersey, your welcome to join me if you like," she said." Jersey didn't move from Sam's side. It made sense, to Annie, that they had bonded so quickly. It made perfect sense to Annie. Sam's voice is soft, and he has a gentle nature about him that animals pick up on right away. "Okay, be that way," laughed Annie as she trotted to her bedroom.

Annie sat on the bed, slipped out of her sneakers, and pulled off her jeans. *This has been the longest day!* She was holding the phone in her hand when she heard a knock. Before she could get off the bed, to open it, the door flew open and there stood Sam and Jersey.

Annie went to grab for something to cover up, although she wasn't quite sure why. This is the way their relationship has been since almost day one. One knock on the door, and no one opens the door. Well, you walk in. But Annie felt as though things were different now. She felt the gaze of Sam's eyes tracing every part of the body: separately. *It was as though I am the pizza, and Sam is Jersey.* Annie had to laugh at the comparison. However, she couldn't deny that she was, in fact, flattered. Jersey jumped up on the bed and snuggled up to her side. Sam followed behind him, landing on the bed just inches away from her. "Well, then I guess we are all going to have a chat with Mom tonight," she said, smiling.

Annie's dad picked up after the first ring. "Where's Mom?" Annie asked abruptly. She wasn't sure why she always asked her dad that question. She just did. Annie could hear mother in the background—asking who was on the phone.

"Hey, Kitten! How are things going," asked her dad?" Hearing her dad call her that caused her to smile. She hadn't heard him call her that, for quite some time. It gave her a good feeling. She felt a reconnection to him that she hadn't felt in a while. Annie and her dad were close, while she was growing up. Of course, her moving away not only put a physical distance between them but an emotional one as well.

"Well said, Annie, things are going okay. Sam and I have agreed to dog sit, for a friend, until Sunday. His name is Jersey, and he is a Puggle too. He is much larger than Molly and a very good boy. How is my little girl doing? I miss her so much."

"She is doing great. We are trying not to spoil her too much, but you know that's nearly impossible," he chuckled. "She is sitting here on my lap. Would you like to talk to her?

Annie didn't hesitate, "Hey baby girl, are you being good

for Grandma and Grandpa? Do you miss us?" Annie could hear dad in the background giggle. When he got back on the phone, he said Molly was doing the head tilt. She knew exactly who it was, and he said Molly was happy to hear Annie's voice.

"Okay, Dad, I'm going to hang up now. I love you and give my love to Mom!" Sam shouted out a goodbye to Annie's dad as she ended the call.

Sam patted Jersey on the head. "I'm going to hit the hay Annie, it's been a long day, and I'm whooped." Annie nodded her head in agreement. It had been a long day.

As Sam was leaving, he suggested to Annie. "Since Jersey is staying with us now, I think it would be a good idea if we cancelled the dinner reservations and had the dinner here, at the apartment. It's going to be difficult to find someone that we know and trust to sit with him, especially last minute. "

Annie didn't hesitate to respond. "Agreed, let's have it here. This little guy has been through enough. I don't see any reason that we can't just have the party here?"

"Party? I didn't know we were having a party."

Annie laughed and waved for him to go. He was halfway to his bedroom when he heard Annie yell, "I'll call tomorrow and change the reservations from sit-in to Cater. I have no plan to cook, Sam!"

—◆—

CHAPTER 10

A Trip to the Dog Park

The following day, Annie woke up to Jersey kissing her face. She knew precisely what that meant, and she didn't bother to resist. "What's the matter, Big guy? Are you ready to start our day?" Annie grabbed her robe from the back of the door, wrapping it around her. The two of them headed out to the kitchen. Annie looked around the apartment, but she didn't see Sam. She saw a paper lying on the table. It was a note from Sam stating that he was going to run a few errands this morning and would be back later, mentioning that when he returned, they would take Jersey to the dog park.

Annie smiled at Jersey, "It looks like we are going to the doggy park later on today!" She grabbed Jersey's food from the pantry. She was thankful that he didn't require the same home-made food as Molly had been accustomed to. Annie watched as Jersey devoured his food. It was gone seconds after she poured it. She wondered if he was getting enough to eat, but judging from his size, he didn't appear to be malnourished at all.

Annie ran back into her bedroom, throwing on yesterday's jeans and an old tee shirt. She slid her feet into her sneakers that she had left by the door, last night. "Come on, big guy, let's get you outside to do your business before you have an accident."

This was the part Annie hated the most, the trips down the elevator and out the back door for Jersey to do his business. *Why does this elevator take so long to open? I just want to get down and back without running into anyone I know; people are not used to seeing me in tee shirts and sneakers. I would like to keep it that way.*

When the door finally opened Annie grabbed Jersey's leash and dashed to hop on while the door was still open. She stepped inside and suddenly felt extremely uncomfortable. There were three men, in dark business suits and loud ties, already in the elevator. Annie spotted Sally's husband. She hadn't seen him since the wedding. *Oh, please don't let him recognize me!* Suddenly she felt insecure and self-conscious. Normally she would be dressed in her professional work attire and would feel confident, and sexy. *Why does he have to be on the elevator today when I'm dressed in yesterday's jeans, an old tee shirt and sneakers?* Annie was certain his wife Sally would never be caught in public looking like this. Just as the elevator reached the ground floor, Annie felt a tap on her shoulder. With a startled look, she turned around.

"Annie Jones! I haven't seen you in such a long time. I barely recognized you. You look so different." Annie smiled, even though, deep down, she wanted to run and hide. The man held his hand out, "I'm sorry, I just assumed you would remember me. I'm Tom Murdoch, we met a few years ago—when Sally and I got married."

"Tom, Hi! Yes, of course, I remember you. How have you been? How is Sally? I haven't seen her in a while."

"Sam tells me you're throwing a party this Saturday at your place?" Tom went on— ignoring her last statement.

"Sam told you that?"

"Oh yes, I saw him at the gym this morning, and he invited me to your party."

Annie laughed. "Well, I guess I should stop referring to it as a party, people are going to get the wrong idea. It's really just a small get-together, one last chance to visit with our friends before we say goodbye to them and New York. I'm so glad you can come. We'll see you Saturday!" Annie gave Jersey's leash a little tug, and off they trotted to the small area behind the building.

Annie was lost in thought as she stood outside waiting for Jersey to relieve himself. *Interesting, when Tom said Sam had invited him to the party, he never mentioned Sally? I guess I'll find out why on Saturday.*

Annie led Jersey to the building's back door, hoping they could sneak back to the apartment— this time without being noticed. She was relieved to find the elevator empty. She watched the door close and let out a sigh of relief. Seconds later the two were in the apartment. *Sometimes it's nice not to be noticed. Huh, where did that come from?*

"Jersey, I'm going to grab a shower, you stay here, and I'll be right back." As Annie walked toward the bathroom, Jersey followed. Annie chuckled, "Okay, Jersey, you can come in and lay on the floor while I shower." Annie closed the door behind him, and she watched as he plopped himself on the floor. She felt a tug at her heart. She couldn't help but wonder if this was a routine for him and his mom before she became sick. Annie was stepping out of the shower and heard her cell phone ringing. She quickly wrapped a towel around her midsection and dashed to the kitchen—where she had left it. Just as Annie reached for her phone, she let out a scream holding her chest as though she were about to have a heart attack.

"Jesus!" Yelled Annie. "You scared me half to death!"

All Sam could do was laugh. "It's not like I purposely set out to scare you, Annie. When I got back, you were in the shower. I just assumed Jersey was in there with you." Annie didn't need to confirm Jersey's whereabouts; he was already at her heels. She checked the missed call, it was from her dad. She dialed up the number right away, in case something was wrong.

Annie's dad answered on the first ring. "Hey, Dad," said Annie in a cheerful voice.

"Hey, Kitten!" responded Annie's dad. *Annie never grew tired of hearing the nickname, Kitten.*

"I was just calling to check in and see how things were going?"

"Things are going great Dad, I just got out of the shower so maybe I can give you a call back later?"

"Sure! Sounds good," he said. "Do you want to say goodbye to Molly first? I am sure she misses you." After a few moments of Annie chatting into Molly's ear about how much she loved her and would see her soon, she said her goodbyes and hung up the phone. Annie couldn't believe it was noon already.

"Did you get my note? I thought we could take Jersey to the dog park today?" said Sam. Annie wasn't sure if Sam was smiling because he was becoming quite fond of Jersey or because she was still standing, in the kitchen, half-naked. She guessed the latter. She couldn't help but laugh at the way Sam stared at her. It was as if he could see through the towel, she had on, and he was admiring her naked body. She found it interesting that Sam didn't bother to hide his attraction to her but instead went out of his way to let her know he was looking.

"Okay, Sam, if we are going to go, we should leave soon. I want to be there before it gets too crowded. Don't forget, we have to start packing later this afternoon."

She rushed to her bedroom to get dressed. She shut the bedroom and quivered. Sam's attraction to her had sent heat waves through her body. She wasn't sure how long she could keep these feelings at bay. It was becoming exceedingly difficult for Annie to deny that she found Sam alluring. Her attraction to Sam was becoming a problem, that she didn't really know how to handle. She knew that if she decided to act on these feelings, their relationship would be forever changed. *Maybe I should just act on my feelings. At least then I wouldn't need to wonder anymore. Maybe I should just do what I want to and let the chips fall where they may.*

Annie went to her closet, picking out a pair of her favorite shorts, a low v cut blouse that hugged her breasts—and accentuated their size. Annie remembered Sam commenting on the low-cut shirt the last time she wore it. She smiled at the memory. *Why am I going through all this trouble to get more of Sam's attention, is this about me or about Sam?* She finished getting dressed, pulled back her hair, and grabbed her jean jacket in case it got chilly.

Annie wasn't at all surprised at the reaction, she got from Sam, as she walked into the living room—with her breast leading the way. His reaction caused her to push them out even more. She loved this attention she was getting from Sam. It was new, exciting, and she hoped he never stopped looking at her like that— like a piece of candy he wanted to savor in his mouth. She could almost see that Sam was ready to burst. "Annie Jones, you really are a tease!" Annie pretended not to have any idea what Sam was talking about. She smiled, shrugged her shoulders, and bent over to slip on her sneakers.

The cool air helped to cool their jets as they walked along. Sam couldn't keep his eyes off her, and she loved every minute of it. Jersey was leading the way in a friendly- calm manner. He looked so proud leading the pack.

They had almost reached the dog park when Annie heard someone call out her name. "Annie Jones!" They turned and spotted Sally jogging towards them, from across the street. Sally leaned in to give Annie a kiss on the cheek, but before she landed it, Sally spotted Sam. "Oh my god!!" Sally yelled. "Sam Lee, I haven't seen you in such a long time!" Annie, still bracing for the kiss that never was, found Sally's excitement to be over the top and slightly irritating. Classic Sally. What happened next had Annie raging inside. She watched as Sally practically knocked Sam over lunging and throwing her arms around his neck and kissing him on the lips. Annie found the whole show sickening: almost laughable. She watched as Sam backed up, escaping Sally's clutch.

Once they had returned to safe talking distance, they chatted about Sally's ex-husband, Tom. Obviously, Sam knew a lot more about Sally and Tom's relationship than she did. Then it happened; "Sam, I heard that you invited Tom to your dinner party on Saturday? I assume the invite is extended to yours, truly? You know how I love dinner parties!" Sally continued to latch onto Sam's arm as she giggled her way into an invite.

"Sure!" said Sam. "Annie and I would be happy to have you!"

"Great!" shouted Sally, "I'll see you Saturday then!" Annie watched as Sally jogged away. *Now I remember why you and I haven't stayed close, like a Poodle in heat, Sally was always self-absorbed.* They watched Sally disappear. He looked for words to explain what had just transpired, but Annie waved her hand at him. She was witness to it all. She watched Sally throwing herself at Sam and he the innocent bystander doing his best to keep his distance while remaining polite. *Sam was always polite.*

The afternoon went by quickly as they watched Jersey playing with the other dogs. Today was Julee's surgery. Annie never asked what time the surgery would be and had no idea if the surgery had even happened yet. She decided she would give Kevin a call later that evening and check on how things went.

Annie had sent Julee photos of Jersey last night to reassure her that he was in good hands. She wasn't sure how much information Kevin had relayed to Julee, so Annie made sure that she did. Annie couldn't imagine strangers caring for Molly if she were ever in that situation and wanted to do her best to reassure Julee that Jersey was doing great and that they were happy to have him.

Annie had to drag Sam and Jersey away from the park. She reminded Sam of their agreement to pack boxes when they returned to the apartment. At last, Sam agreed to leave, and Jersey led the way back to the apartment complex. *It was almost as though he knew where they were going.*

CHAPTER 11

The Plan to Extend the Apartment's Lease

That evening, before going to bed, Annie made a list of the things that needed to be done and left it lying on the counter. The following day she pulled out the list and began reading it to Sam.

"Sam, we need to come up with a menu for Saturday's dinner. I'll call the restaurant this afternoon and simply make the change. How many people do you plan on having here?"

Sam shrugged his shoulders, "I don't really have an exact number. I invited some of my friends and coworkers casually, sort of an open invitation, you know? I'm quite sure there will be at least five, but it could be as many as fifteen."

Annie's eyes grew wide, "Sam, you're joking, right? How can we plan a dinner if we don't even know who or how many people are coming?"

Sam shrugged his shoulders again. "Annie, why do you

insist on making such a big deal out of everything? Even things that are supposed to be fun. You find a way to make them unbearable, just relax."

"Well, Sam, here you go. Here's the menu and phone number for the restaurant. You figure out what we will be having for dinner and how much you should order!" Annie stormed off. "I have invited five people from work."

"Come on, Jersey, we are going to pack!" Jersey followed Annie down the hall— looking back to see if Sam was coming.

Annie didn't waste any time. She began taping boxes and removing and packing items from the top of her dresser. She started with jewelry box, a set of candles, and a bottle of her favorite perfume. She began wrapping the jewelry box, in some newspaper, when she heard Sam's phone ring. She stopped to listen. She heard Sam talking. She was sure it was Kevin. She needed to know how Julee's surgery went. She was concerned for both Julee and Jersey's well-being. She didn't wait for Sam to come into the bedroom. She walked into the living room with Jersey in tow. Annie made eye contact with Sam and tilted her head, with a look of concern. She was unaware that Jersey, now standing beside her, was looking at Sam the same way. Seeing this, Sam couldn't help but smile. He gave Annie a reassuring nod and she knew the surgery had gone well.

Annie let out a sigh of relief. Sam ended the call and reached for Annie. He pulled her into his arms and hugged her. Annie could feel the tears welling up into her eyes. She didn't know why she was crying, but the tears flowed until she was in a full-blown sob. Sam remained silent and hugged her even tighter. He didn't bother to ask why—he just held her. He stroked her hair while kissing forehead. Time just stood still as she pulled herself, tightly into his chest. He gently separated himself from her as he looked her directly into her eyes, "I love you, Annie Jones!" This time Annie didn't hold back. She didn't stop to think about the what-ifs or if what she knew was about to happen was a good idea. Annie looked up, staring into Sam's eyes, and she responded, I love you too, Sam Lee! I love you so much, and I am so sorry for the way things have been."

Sam gently grabbed Annie's mouth and kissed her. She didn't pull away this time, but instead, she invited him to her mouth, her lips swelled with desire. Annie had dreamt of this moment for months now. She wanted Sam as badly as he wanted her. She had to give in. She couldn't pretend any longer. Annie found herself lost in his essence. She was ready to give herself up to him, freely, prepared for anything Sam was willing to give.

Suddenly there was a knock on the door. At first, they both tried to ignore it. This the moment was a long time coming and now that it was here, they did not want it to end. "I suppose I should answer the door," said Sam. He kissed Annie one more time and went to the door—trying to gather his composure.

Sam walked over and opened the door. Annie could tell that he was irritated.

"Hey, Joe! What brings you back here on this delightful day?" Annie could hear Joe's stuttering.

"Well, I thought we could continue our conversation, from the other day. I am ready to show the apartment, and you still have not given me final conformation on when you plan to vacate."

Sam sounded angry when he responded. "Well, Joe, Annie, and I haven't made the final decision yet, but when we do, you'll be the first to know."

By now, Annie was standing at the door, alongside Sam— glaring at Joe.

Sam didn't bother to wait for Joe to respond as he closed the door abruptly.

"The guy has got some nerve, Annie. We told him we would get back to him!"

Annie knew the moment was over, and she knew he was just as disappointed she was.

Sam walked toward the kitchen, as he called out to Annie, "While I was out this morning, I stopped by the sandwich shop and grabbed us both a turkey on rye. Annie didn't hesitate to respond. If there was one thing, she missed about New York it was the delicious and readily available food available on nearly every block.

Sam brought the sandwiches in and sat down. Annie couldn't help but grin when she saw the third plate with a small sandwich arranged in tiny triangles. Sam sat it on the coffee table alongside theirs. "This one is for you Jersey boy." Annie could see Jersey's eyes grow wide, he knew what Sam was saying, and he was excited.

"Jersey is such good boy," said Annie. "I wish we could keep him. It's going to be hard to say goodbye to him Sunday." Sam nodded his head in agreement. They both had become very fond of Jersey in such a short amount of time.

"Sam, I am not sure I want to bring this up, but when you told Joe that we hadn't made our decision yet, were you being honest?" Sam didn't respond. He was too busy feeding Jersey pieces of the sandwich. "Sam, please answer me," said Annie.

Annie rambled on as though Sam had responded. "Sam, this is our last chance. I want to keep the apartment for at least another six months. You know they plan to raise the rent to an ungodly amount, and what if?" Sam didn't hesitate to jump in.

"What if what? Annie, what were you going to say? Do you think we won't make it as roommates now that our life has been forever changed? Or are you saving the apartment for me, just in case it doesn't work out, so I would have a place to come back to?" Annie waited as Sam continued to talk.

"Sam, I love you. I have no doubt that we are going to be fine together. But I want a place to return to in the summer—when we decide we want to do more than sit on the porch and look at one another." Sam couldn't help but laugh. He knew Annie was right. They have lived in New York for so long, it was impossible to think of a life without ever returning.

"We were lucky enough to get this place when we did, and the rent was reasonable. We can afford to keep it, at least for six months, until the contract comes up again. It would cost us almost as much to get out of the lease early as it would to keep the place."

Sam nodded his head in agreement. It wouldn't make any sense to pull out of the contract now. They should just wait and see. Annie tried not to let Sam see her excitement. Deep down, she couldn't bear the thought of giving up the apartment. But, baby-steps, she reminded herself. This was going to take some time.

Annie grabbed the paper plates from the coffee table and walked into the kitchen. "Sam, have you ordered the food for the dinner party yet?" When he didn't respond, she knew the answer right away. "Sam, you need to get the order placed and soon. I don't want people showing up here, with nothing to feed them.

Annie grabbed the menu from the counter. "Okay, Sam, they have made it simple. Appetizers, Entrees, and dessert. Pick what you like and be sure to order enough food for everyone you have invited." Annie handed him his cell phone and walked to her bedroom. She didn't want any part of it.

—◆—

CHAPTER 12

Annie's Surprise Talk with Kevin

Annie sat on her bed, looking around the room. *Well at least we don't have to pack up everything we own right now. We have the next six months to get it done. What about the U-Haul? We should get that returned right away.* She felt a sigh of relief. Annie hated packing, and the idea of giving up the apartment caused her too much anxiety.

Annie could hear Sam on the phone speaking with the restaurant manager. *He is always so pleasant. It sounds like he is ordering everything they had on their menu. Finally, Sam has realized what I have been saying all along. It's impossible to plan food for a dinner party when you don't how many guests are coming. But that was his problem now.*

Sam finished the food order and made his way towards Annie's bedroom. She could hear his footsteps getting closer. She felt panicked yet excited at the same time. She wondered if he planned to pick up where they left off a few hours ago? Sam didn't say a word as he entered her bedroom and laid down next to her. Jersey followed behind, jumping on the bed and landing between the two of them. They both laughed. Jersey was the best boy.

Annie's heart sank when she thought about Jersey's momma and his future. "Sam, what if Julee can't care for Jersey when she gets home? Who do you think he would stay with? I would hope not Kevin and his wife. I mean, he is a nice guy Sam but not capable of caring for Jersey. Jersey is special. Julee cared for him just as we care for Molly." Sam held his head down. Annie could see his sadness.

"It's going to be okay. New York doctors are some of the best in the world. She is in good hands."

Sam stood up and began bouncing on the bed. Jersey was so excited he, of course, had to join in.

"What do you want to do now?" Sam yelled. Jersey barked while Sam jumped. Annie was laughing so hard as Sam pulled her to her feet so she could join in. There they were—Sam and Annie; jumping on the bed, feeling alive again feeling as though nothing had changed between them. But Annie knew the truth, things had changed between them, and that this was just one fleeting moment and as soon as the moment was over, things would go back to the way they were. *I love Sam, I love him now more than ever. I just don't know how to tell him that I am ready to move on with him in a romantic way. If I tell Sam, I love him as more than a friend, he is going to propose again. I don't know if I am ready to commit to marriage. We have never had sex before! How could I agree to marry someone I have never had sex with?* Annie dismissed the thoughts from her mind—She was enjoying the moment. She noticed herself feeling even more drawn to Sam, as she watched him. She loved how his curly hair bounced as he jumped up and down. She loved the smell of his cologne and his strong- masculine body. She couldn't help but feel attracted to him. The flirting moments they had shared in the past few days only added to her desire for him.

Then it happened. Annie felt the impact right before she heard the sound. It was the sound of the wooden bed frame snapping beneath them. She grabbed ahold of Sam's arm as they tumbled onto the mattress that now lay on the shattered bedframe. Annie laughed when she saw the horror in Jersey's eyes. She rushed over to him and reassure him that everything was okay. "It's just a little mishap," Annie told him, as she patted his head. Sam stood up, from the bed, and tried to get a better look at their dilemma. "Well, Annie Jones, if we can't fix it, you can always sleep in my room. Annie didn't know how to respond, so she smiled and winked. This wasn't the first time that Sam had left her speechless.

"Don't worry, Annie, I can fix it," said Sam. She could hear the clanking of tools from the other room. She decided it was best if she and Jersey just stay where they were. She sat on the floor as Jersey snuggled up tightly to her side. They sat in silence with Annie petting Jersey's back—reassuring him that everything was okay. Loud noises frightened Jersey and Annie understood that. Sam returned with a smile on his face and several tools placed in his arms. *He obviously had a plan. Look out!*

"Annie, why don't you take Jersey outside while I put your bed back together. The noise is going to frighten him, even more, once I begin using the drill."

Annie nodded in agreement. "Come on, Jersey, let's take a walk outside!" The two of them walked toward the front door, and Annie grabbed his leash from the hook. "You really are ready to get out of here, aren't you, buddy?" Jersey let out one quick bark—in agreement.

Annie took ahold of the lead, and off they went. She and Jersey moved quickly, to the back door, in hopes of avoiding other tenants. Annie knew Sam would need some time to fix the bed.

Annie sat on the bench and drifted off in thought. *When is the right time to let my guard down with Sam? What would have happened if Joe hadn't shown up when he did? Would we have made love, and if we had, then what? Would Sam expect us to get married, to have kids?*

Annie was startled when she heard a voice behind her. "I'm sorry, Annie, I didn't mean to scare you. I saw you walk out the back door with Jersey. I wanted to catch up to you, in person, and let you know about Julee."

Annie patted on the bench for Kevin to sit down, "Kevin, I am sorry your sister is going through this. You look awful. You look—like you haven't eaten in days. If there is anything else we could do, to help, please let us know."

"Annie, my sister is resting comfortably now. The doctors want to do more testing—to be sure she is out of danger. It looks like her hospital stay will be a little longer than anticipated. I know this is a lot to ask Annie, but please stay in New York for just a few days longer. I need to be there for her and, I know that Jersey is in good hands. We are the only family each of us has."

"I have an idea that is sure to put a smile on Julee's face today. Why don't you squat down by Jersey, and I'll snap a picture? Julee will have a moment of peace when she's sees

Jersey smiling face. She has been worried. Julee could never have kids. After her divorce from her husband, she rescued Jersey from an abusive home, and they have been together ever since."

Annie squatted down by Jersey. She thought for a moment. Staying here another few days meant being away from Molly even longer. She knew Molly was in good hands, but she missed her. Annie shook her head as if to dismiss the thought for at least a moment. This moment was about Jersey and his mom: Julee. Kevin wanted to capture the relationship that Annie and Jersey had on film and send it to his sister. Annie sat cross-legged and wrapped her arms tightly around Jersey. She wanted to make sure they got a good picture for Julee. Kevin smiled, "Julee is going to love these pictures."

Annie looked up into the sky, she saw a large black cloud headed their way. She was sure she felt a few raindrops. "Kevin, we should get going. The sky is going to let loose us soon." Kevin nodded in agreement.

"Look Kevin I will talk to Sam and let you know," Within moments, the sky opened, and it began to downpour—sending them all running for cover. Annie darted for the back door with Jersey. Thankfully, she was able to close the door just in time— saving them both from getting drenched. They both scurried to the elevator and back to the apartment. She hoped that Sam had finished fixing her bed and she wouldn't be faced with that dilemma tonight.

Annie pushed the door open. There stood Sam to greet them.

"You're just in time, Annie. Your bed is as good as new. I expect it can withstand whatever activities you may have planned in the future," said Sam—as he gave her a little wink. Annie couldn't help but chuckle. Sam always did flirt with her but in a fun-loving way. She never took him seriously, although now she knew better. She decided the moment he kissed her that she was ready to take things to the next level. She was tired of ignoring her feelings. She was tantalized by his scent. She was taunted by his lean-sexy body. His eyes and his charming smile captivated her. If Sam wasn't the one, there was only going to be one way to find out.

"Annie, I tried to call Kevin, but all I got was his voicemail." Annie had been so caught up in her moment of lust that she forgot to mention that she had seen Kevin. She explained everything to Sam. She told him how Kevin had asked that they stay in New York for another few days—until Julee was released from the hospital. She was surprised by Sam's lack of immediate response. He nodded his head as if to agree with everything she said. And then, with a quick turn of his body to face Jersey, he said, "Well, Pal, looks like you are stuck with us for a few more days!"

Annie spoke up as quickly as she could before he changed his mind. "Sam, we still have Molly at my parent's house. I'll give them a call and ask them to keep her for a few more days. If they say no, I will need to go back, and you can stay here with Jersey."

Sam had already reached out to Chet to have him return the U-Haul. He planned to rent a small SUV for their return trip. They could easily fit their belongings into a much smaller vehicle— now that they have decided to hold onto the apartment.

Annie walked into her bedroom and dialed her mom's number. Once again, it was her father who answered. "Hi Dad, where is Mom?" *She wasn't sure why she always asked the same question when her father answered the phone instead of her mother?*

Annie's dad responded in his usual cheerful voice. "Your mom and Aunt Alice went on a little shopping trip, for the day. Alice has been lonely without Jack being around. She called your mom the other day, to see if she would like to go shopping, and of course, your mom said yes. How is New York? Did you get everything packed up in one U-Haul, or will there be a fleet of them driving through town," he asked? They both laughed. Annie knew what her father was insinuating. Annie did love to shop. Luckily, Sam was a minimalist and did his best to keep their apartment simple and uncluttered. Annie stuck to buying clothes for herself most of the time anyway.

"Dad, we have been asked to stay here in New York for a few more days. Jersey's human mom is still in the hospital, and they want to run more tests, before releasing her. Is that going to be a problem? If it is, I can come home, and Sam will stay here until Julee is released."

Annie's dad laughed, "Well if we keep this sweet little girl much longer, we may not give her back when you do return!" Annie knew that was her father speaking for himself. Her mother was not typically an animal person.

Annie's dad put the phone to Molly's ear so she could hear Annie's voice. Annie spoke softly. "We miss you, baby girl. We will be home soon—with some new toys. You be a good girl."

Annie knew her dad was joking when he said he may not give Molly back. "I'm fine with Molly staying on with us for a few more days and to be quite honest, your mom has become a huge Molly fan as well. You take your time; we love and miss you both."

"I will talk to you soon, Dad. Tell Mom I said hello and send her our love." Annie ended the call and found herself missing Molly more than ever. She stretched out on her bed.

She could hear Sam clanking pans around in the kitchen. *I wonder what he is up to now.* It wasn't long before she could smell garlic and onion. Apparently, Sam was cooking tonight. Annie rolled off the bed and headed for the kitchen. "Sam, I'm not sure what you have cooking in that pan, but it smells amazing."

"Go sit down and keep Jersey occupied. I have tripped over him three times already I guess he thinks it smells amazing too," laughed Sam.

Annie laughed even louder, "Well, that's because Jersey knows what smells good, usually tastes even better."

Annie walked over to the cupboard and pulled out two wine glasses. It was common practice for them to keep at least a few bottles of wine on hand, and she was sure she would find at least one unopened bottle— tucked away, and that she did. It was a Napa Valley Cabernet. Sam had received this bottle of wine as a Christmas gift, from one of his clients, last year. It was a much higher end wine than they would typically have on hand, but Annie thought tonight was the perfect time to open it. She held it in the air as if to ask Sam for his approval. Sam gave her an approving nod. "I love the way you think, Annie Jones!" Annie smiled. She loved it when Sam called her that. She had no idea why, but she did, and he knew it. There were a lot of things Sam knew about Annie, and she loved that about him.

CHAPTER 13

Things Heat Up before the Dinner Party

The next day, was consumed with preparations for the dinner party. Annie had given Sam a list of items that would need to be picked up from the store. Annie ran around the apartment, rearranging furniture and just getting ready. She knew she was going overboard. They hadn't lived in the apartment for a few months, and it had been professionally cleaned while they were in Texas.

Then the day finally arrived, it was the day of the party. Sam and Annie hit the ground running. There were a lot of preparations that needed to be done, for Sam's little party. Even though Annie did not have much interest in the whole thing, she wanted to make sure the party was a good one. She, for whatever reason, knew it was important to Sam. She wanted to do something nice for the guy that was always there for her. *Well at least I won't have to clean. I'm glad we had the apartment cleaned while we were in Murphy.*

Annie had made her way to the kitchen. She caught a glimpse of Jersey, sitting in the middle of the living room— watching her. She smiled at him and walked into the room to be closer to him. "Oh, Jersey, you're such a good boy. It's going to be hard to give you up when your momma gets better." Jersey looked at her with his big brown eyes. *Jersey looks sad today.* "Jersey boy, are you okay?" asked Annie. She sat down beside him, on the floor, and stroked his back. Within seconds he was on his back waiting for a good old-fashioned belly rub. Annie couldn't help but laugh— he had her right where he wanted her. At least she was sure there was nothing wrong with him. He was just a little lonely and needed some attention. "Okay, a few more moments, and then I must get things ready for tonight. Are you ready for tonight, Jersey?" Annie hadn't given much thought to how Jersey would feel about being around a bunch of strangers. *Well, Sam and I were strangers to the little hulk just a few short days ago. I think he'll be fine.*

"Well, Jersey, Kevin, and his wife will be here tonight. At least you will know them." "Okay, buddy, I have work to do. Lucky for you, your only job is to sit and look cute, just like you are doing." Annie smiled as she pulled her hand away from Jersey's belly and pushed herself onto her feet.

Just as Annie was bringing herself to her feet, Sam walked in. His arms were loaded with bags. Annie couldn't help but wonder how he even carried it all? She ran over to help him get into the apartment and closed the door. The bags had become an entangled mess around his arms. Annie knew the best thing she could do was rush to the kitchen and make room, on the counter, for the bags.

Annie listened as Sam ranted about the stores and streets being so crowded. He was annoyed at the way people pushed by him, as if he didn't exist. Annie smiled, "Sam, those people haven't changed—you have."

Sam had a puzzled look on his face. "Perhaps you're right," he said. He continued to unpack the bags—still not sure what Annie meant.

The only thing Annie could think about, right now, was the moment he brushed up against her. She felt hungry for his kiss, again. The kind of kiss that told her she was the only one for him. The sort of kiss he gave her just a few short days ago—before they were so rudely interrupted. *Where is that, Sam?* Annie shook her head. She wanted to dismiss the thought as soon as it came to her. *We are planning a big dinner party tonight, and that was more important than an afternoon rendezvous with the man I am in love with.*

Annie's thoughts were quickly interrupted by the ringing of Sam's phone. "Annie, can you grab that? I want to start preparing the appetizers." Even though Sam had ordered enough food to feed an army, he still had a few of his own favorites that he wanted to make. Annie grabbed Sam's phone from the counter. She didn't recognize the number, so she answered it cautiously.

"Hello," said Annie. She heard a woman's voice on the other end. "Oh, I am sorry, I must have dialed the wrong number. I was looking for Sam Lee."

"This is Annie. Sam asked me to answer his phone for him. May I tell him who is calling?"

"Oh, Annie! I should have guessed, you two always were inseparable. This is Sally!"

Annie felt sick to her stomach and instantly furious. She walked to her bedroom—out of Sam's hearing range.

"First things first Sally. Why are you calling Sam and how did you get his number? Have you forgotten that I know how you are?"

"Excuse me," replied Sally.

"You heard me," snapped Annie.

Annie decided she was going to lie. "I'm sorry he just stepped into the shower. I'll have him call you when he gets out." Annie ended the call abruptly, deleted the number, and laid his phone on the counter.

"Anyone important," Sam asked?

"It was just a solicitor; you know how they are?"

Annie was ashamed of what she had done. But things were going so well between the two of them, she couldn't risk Sally swooping in and changing any of that. Annie walked behind Sam, placing her arms around his midsection. She laid her head on his back—listening to his breath. It was so soothing. Sam let out a groaning sound letting Annie know that he approved.

"Annie Jones, are you trying to distract me," he asked? Annie didn't respond. She was too caught up in her own thoughts to even think about stepping away.

Why did Sally call Sam? How did she get his cell phone number? Is she going to show up here tonight? "Are you okay?" Annie heard the question and struggled to respond.

"Of course, Sam, why wouldn't I be?" Sam shrugged his shoulders. Annie slapped his bottom and laughed as she moved away.

The time was quickly ticking away. "Sam, if you don't require my assistance in the kitchen, I am going to take a shower.

Annie looked at her watch. "Tick-tock, tick-tock," she teased. Sam nodded, and Annie took that as a yes.

Jersey followed Annie into the bathroom. She didn't think much of it. She was used to it by now. Seeing Jersey laying on the floor, reminding Annie how much she missed Molly. Finding out they were going to be staying even longer, broke her heart. *Just a few more days.*

This was going to be an important evening and Annie wanted to be in a good mood for it. She knew that there would be friends and coworkers of Sam's that she hadn't met before. She wanted to create a good impression. Most of all, she wanted to impress Sam.

She chose a black lace dress that fit snug in all the right places. showing off her petite body and accentuating all her physical assets. Annie purchased the dress at a little boutique near the apartment building. At first, she was a little shy about trying it on. She relaxed when the associate raved about how wonderful she looked. She knew then and there that she had to buy it. She knew she made the right choice and was excited to be wearing it. tonight.

Annie stepped out of the shower, and for the first time in months she used the hair dryer and hair straightener to style her hair. She had purchased all new makeup and accessories to draw focus to this dress. Tonight, was a special event and she wanted to be what Sam enjoyed most. When her look was finally completed, she wrapped the towel around herself, and she tiptoed to the bedroom. Surprisingly, Jersey hadn't followed her this time. He must have smelled the food being prepared in the kitchen. Annie laughed to herself. She was thankful that the main dishes were coming from a favorite bistro of theirs and Sam was preparing the appetizers. Certainly,

Jersey didn't mind that it was only appetizers. He did not discriminate!

Annie stepped into her bedroom and closed the door snuggly behind her. She couldn't risk Jersey pushing his way through the door before she had a chance to complete her look. She had left the dress hanging on the inside of her, now open, closet door. She took the dress off the hook and held it up to herself. She smiled as she looked into the full-length mirror. She was glad the sales associate pushed her into buying it. Normally, she would have looked at the display and that's where it would have ended.

Annie smiled. She couldn't wait to see the look on Sam's face— as he first sees her. She was sure he was going to love this dress. It was a lace V-neck that hugged in all the right spots. It was a maxi dress with thin spaghetti straps— revealing Annie's neck and shoulders. A tan sateen material sparingly covered her breasts. The mid and leg section was of the same sateen material— with more lace, allowing for a peekaboo view. *There was no doubt about it, Sam was going to go wild over this dress!*

Annie opted for a neutral color high-heel sandal, with a peekaboo toe. The sales associate helped her pick the shoes out, as well. They really completed the look. There was no doubt, Annie was excited for this evening. She decided the moment she picked out this dress it was going to happen tonight. Annie was going to seduce Sam. She smiled as she looked into the full-length mirror and put on Sam's birthday necklace.

She could hear Sam, in the kitchen, slaving away as he belted out a tune. It reminded her that they did not share the same taste in music. Annie tried to pull herself together.

She felt extremely nervous yet excited. Annie knew that once she and Sam turned that corner, their friendship would be changed forever. Annie imagined what it was going to feel like snuggled into Sam's arms, not as a friend but as his lover. *Sam as my lover? Life sure does have a way of shaking things up.*

Annie took one last look, in the mirror, before she walked toward the kitchen. By the time she made it to the end of the hallway, Sam let out a whistle. She smiled as her heart melted. It was the exact response she was hoping she would get.

"Hey there sexy lady, do you mind telling me what you did with Annie Jones, I watched her walk into that bedroom so she couldn't be far," Sam teased! He didn't bother to wait for Annie to reach him. He met her half-way down the hallway. He grabbed her by the waist and said, "all teasing aside, Annie Jones you look absolutely stunning! If I hadn't already asked you to marry me once before, I would be asking you now." Annie didn't know how to respond to that., but she knew in her heart, if Sam had proposed again, right now, she would say yes, but he didn't. Sam pulled her a little closer. He spotted the necklace and smiled. "Annie, I have always loved this necklace on you, thank you for wearing it." Annie smiled as Sam leaned into her— pushing his lips and body against hers. Her skimpy dress was all that separated them. She was on fire. Annie tried to steady herself as she felt her legs wobble, in her high heels.

"Sam, I need to sit down!" Sam helped her to the kitchen stool. "I am so sorry Sam; I don't know what came over me?"

Sam smiled, "It's called lust Annie Jones and I felt it my-self." Annie smiled; she knew he was right. They both wanted it to happen. They also knew they didn't want to rush it; this was a big step in their relationship. "Jersey, you look after Annie, it's my turn to hit the shower." Annie looked down at Jersey, laying on the kitchen floor. He was never far from where the food happened to be.

Annie was disappointed, yet relieved that Sam had ended their moment. They had guests coming and she needed to concentrate on being an awesome hostess. Annie gathered some platters from the cupboard and began laying out Sam's appetizers. Everything looked and smelled amazing. *This is going to be a great party!*

Annie wasn't sure what time Sam had told people to arrive? She ran to bedroom to grab the wireless phone. *These will be perfect!* Annie heard the water from the shower shut off as she was walking back to the kitchen. She paused in front of the bathroom door. She had so many ideas running through her mind. *I could just go in there and seduce Sam while he was standing in the bathroom naked, but I am already dressed for the party, my dress would get wrinkled, my hair would be a mess and my makeup would smear. All good points, the seduction will have to wait until after the party.* She grabbed the speaker and moved quickly towards the kitchen. She wanted to get the music started before Sam did. Annie opted for something a little less heavy metal and a bit more soothing— Jimmy Buffet, Bryan Adams, Foreigner and Meatloaf. She had all the songs picked out and loaded before Sam even came out. *Mission accomplished.*

Annie heard the bedroom door open. She could feel her heartbeat just a little bit faster. She tried to ignore the fact that her hands were clammy. Instead, she continued putting appetizers on the plate—to avoid looking up. She was too nervous to look up. Sam moved quickly down the hall, and he was already standing next her, when she looked up again. "Ugh Sam, you startled me. I didn't see you coming down the hall." Part of that was a lie and she knew but she didn't care.

"I see you beat me to the playlist of music," chuckled Sam.

Annie nodded. She was caught up in Sam's vibe. The way he smelled, the way he looked. He always wore that same cologne. Sam swirled around the kitchen. "Well, Annie Jones, what do you think of *my* attire?" Annie was afraid to turn around and looked. She knew he was going to look amazingly handsome, and he did. "I did a little shopping myself," he smirked. Annie had to turn around and face him. He put himself on display just for her, she certainly couldn't ignore him. He had no idea that she was ready to jump on him the moment he touched her shoulders and kissed her on the lips an hour ago. Unfortunately for her, she was having a much harder time moving past that moment than he was. Annie turned around. She heard her voice gasp, but she couldn't be sure if the gasp was loud enough for Sam to hear. There he stood, her best friend. Her admirer, the man who proposed to her.

Sam continued to swirl around as though he were on a New York runway. His towel- dried hair lay in a sexy but messy sort of way. Sam kept his hair short above his ears, but the top he kept long enough to allow the curls to run wild. He had only a shadow of a beard. *That's quite a sexy look for you Sam.* A snug white V-neck tee shirt. The sleeves were just short enough to show off the heart tattoo that sat just a few inches above his triceps. "Sam, you look fantastic*!*" *You look better than fantastic. You look incredibly handsome, sexy!*

"Why thank you," Sam smiled. Annie was impressed. She could tell that he was spending more time at time at the gym. Annie didn't bother to look up at Sam—she was sure she didn't want to know if he heard it. "Annie, what do you think of my new jeans?" Annie wondered if Sam was going to tire of swirling around, he certainly didn't look like he was giving up anytime soon. Perhaps Sam knew precisely what was going through Annie's mind, and he was enjoying her reactions more than she was aware.

"I love those jeans!" Annie blurted out.

CHAPTER 14

The Dinner Guests Arrive

Suddenly, a knock on the door. Annie had to regain her composure. She was enjoying the modeling show more than she wanted to admit. She had only wished they weren't planning a dinner party tonight. She convinced herself she could wait a few more hours. Once the dinner party was over, and everyone has gone home—this was going to be their night. Annie was sure of it. Even if she had to be the one to make the first move.

"I'll get that Annie. Why don't you grab some wine glasses from cupboard? In fact, why don't you pour yourself a glass while I answer that?" Annie nodded and walked to the cupboard. They had several styles of wine glasses that they had collected over the years. Annie pulled down her favorite glass, a Swarovski Crystalline wine glass, along with several others and placed them on the counter. She wanted to be as prepared as possible when the other guests arrive. There was a wide array of additional wine bottles tucked away for a rainy day or perhaps tonight, if needed. To Annie's surprise, Kevin and his wife were their first guests. Sam ushered them in and spared no time introducing Annie to Kevin's wife, Kate. Kate smiled as she walked toward Annie and held out her hand to greet her. "I have heard so much about you Annie, I am happy to finally meet you." Annie smiled and pointed, "Kate, this is Jersey." Jersey laid quietly on the floor. Kate looked in Jersey's direction but didn't bother to acknowledge him, this irritated Annie. "Oh yes, I remember Jersey. We have met on a few occasions. We used to visit Kevin's sister Julee occasionally before she became ill," Annie nodded. She knew Kate didn't care much for Jersey. But she was in her home now, Jersey's temporary home, and Kate would have to deal with it. Jersey stood up and walked over toward the two of them as they were talking. Annie didn't pay too much attention, to what he may have been have doing, until she heard Kate shriek! Annie watched Jersey bolt in the other direction. She wasn't sure what had happened. "Goddamn you Jersey, you just peed in my purse!" Annie snickered, on the inside, but was very apologetic "I am so sorry Kate, Jersey has never peed on anything before." Annie rushed to get a napkin from the kitchen, but Kate was already on her way to the bathroom—purse in her hand. "Jersey that was naughty," scolded Annie! As much as she thought Kate probably deserved it, she couldn't let him go around peeing wherever he wanted. Kate returned to the kitchen after cleaning her purse. Annie smiled at her and once again apologized for Jersey's behavior. Kate sat down at the counter and Annie offered her a glass of wine. *The wine is going down too smoothly tonight, and it is still quite early.* "A glass of wine sounds wonderful, Annie. I do like a cabernet." Annie smiled as she poured the wine. Jersey's dislike of Kate only reinforced Annie's opinion.

The guests continued to arrive, and the tiny apartment began filling up quickly. Sam was speaking with an older gentleman—that Annie didn't recognize. He motioned for Annie to join them just as the doorbell rang. She answered the door—leaving Sam to his conversation.

"Oh, Sally. What a pleasant surprise. I wasn't expecting you here tonight?" Annie had to force herself to smile. Deep down she was angry. She was angry that Sam had invited her in the first place and even more angry knowing that Sally had eyes for Sam. She was never shy about her feelings, especially when it came to men. *You have got some nerve Sally waltzing in here like some Poodle in heat expecting Sam to grovel at your feet. He may not see what you're up to, but you're not fooling me!*

There was no doubt that even on a bad day, Sally was drop dead gorgeous. It was in her genes—and her jeans. She had a very athletic body. Most women would spend hours at gym trying to imitate her look. Even her jet-black hair, showed no sign of graying, it was flawless. Annie was convinced that Sally had to be dying. *Nobody's hair is that black—naturally. I wonder what else is artificial.*

Sally was dressed just as Annie would have expected her to be dressed. Her skimpy black dress that covered only the nipples of her breasts and barely covered her backside. Her black stiletto heels gave her legs a long slender look. She was dressed to impress. *Oh yes, Sally was on a mission tonight.* Sally was not shy about her body, in fact, Annie was sure that tonight she was going out of her way to get Sam's attention. *Over my dead body!*

Annie stood staring at Sally as if she were a goddess that had fallen from the sky, showing up at their doorstep—to ruin Annie's night.

Sally reached out, touching Annie's arm. "Aren't you going to let me in Annie?" Annie didn't know what to say. She was feeling conflicted. She wanted to tell her to go away, tell her there was no party, and tell her Sam was not here. Sally spotted Sam and pushed her way past Annie— headed straight toward him. Annie closed the door, trying to regain her composure. *Things were going so well, why oh why did she have to show up here?*

Annie decided right then and there, she was not going to let Sally get in the way of her and Sam's evening. She had a plan, and she was going to stick with it—even if that meant playing Sally's game. *I can be just as seductive and manipulating as Sally can be.* Annie closed the door and scanned the apartment. A woman asked Annie where the bathroom was, and she pointed her down the hall. Annie's eyes locked on to Sally. *I am not taking my eyes off from you tonight.* Annie worked her way to the other side of the room—weaving her way through the crowd. Annie was polite. She excused herself as she made her way through. Sally simply pushed her way through the crowd because she was somehow more important than anything that happened to stand in her way.

Annie watched Sam's expressions as he spoke with Sally. She eagerly searched his eyes to see if he showed any sign of interest. She had a sigh of relief, she was sure Sally would take Sam's politeness as a sign of interest, but Sam didn't look at Sally the way he looked at Annie. Sally stood there with her hand on Sam's arm—rubbing it up and down. Annie knew what Sally was up to. *This isn't going to work out the way you think, Sally dear.*

Sam spotted Annie, heading in their direction, and waved for her to come over. Annie nodded. *I am moving as fast as I can. I know what is at stake. Sam must sense that Sally might have other intentions and perhaps he is calling on me to rescue him. or he could just be oblivious to Sally's flirting and sucking it up just like all those other men in the past.* Annie couldn't remember a time when she had so much hatred for a woman. A woman who used to be her best friend.

—◆—

CHAPTER 15

Annie is Sparked with Jealousy

You're not angry, you're jealous and worried. It's not Sally's fault you turned down Sam's proposal. It is also not Sally's fault that she's drop dead gorgeous and has eyes for your best friend. Sally doesn't even know that you are attracted to Sam, let alone that you love him.

Annie knew everything she was thinking was true, and she knew that she had to save Sam from Sally. Annie was breathing hard by the time she reached the two of them. Sally looked at Annie in an odd way, "Are you okay Annie, you seem a little out of breath?"

"No, no, no I'm fine. It was just a little challenging maneuvering through the crowd." Sally nodded.

"Don't worry Annie, I am taking good care of Sam. We were just catching up on old times." Annie gave Sally a fake smile. She felt sick to her stomach. She had to make sure that nothing happened between Sam and Sally tonight. The question was, how was she going to do that?

Sam spotted an old colleague of his and excused himself from the conversation. Sally looked crushed but Annie she was relieved. She wasn't sure how she would keep up this game all night, but she knew she must.

Sally stuck around for a few more minutes making small talk with Annie. She tried, unsuccessfully, to hide the fact that she was just trying to find out what kind of relationship Sam and Annie had. She thought about telling Sally that she and Sam were engaged but soon thought better. She knew one lie would just lead to another, and she doubted that, that, would stop Sally, anyway. "Thank you for coming to tonight. Sam and I wanted to have a chance to say goodbye before we packed up our stuff and headed back home. As I mentioned before, Sam and I have a place in my hometown, Murphy, Texas." Annie smiled as she watched Sally's eyes grow wide. *Mission accomplished; You don't have much time for anything you might be planning.*

"Annie what is your deal with Sam?" Sally asked. Annie tried to respond non- chaleantly, "Sam is my best friend, Sally." Sally nodded and smiled. Unfortunately for Annie, that meant Sam was fair game tonight and once again she only had herself to blame.

Annie excused herself from their conversation. She decided another glass of wine would be needed, if she was going to get through this dinner party. She was happy for Sam. All the party planning and preparation seemed to be paying off. Everything was going splendidly—Sam was having a good time. It wasn't often they had dinner parties and certainly not one this size. Everyone seemed to be enjoying themselves.

Annie scoured the room for Sam as she walked toward the kitchen. She caught a glimpse of him standing next to Joe, the apartment manager. Annie shook her head. She couldn't believe Sam would invite him—considering how badly he had treated them. Annie watched Sam. He was always so relaxed, no matter what the occasion. Even dinner parties didn't get him anxious or nervous. He knew he would have it under control and he did. Annie watched as he moved his hands around while talking to Joe. She wasn't sure what they were talking about, but she was sure it was guy stuff. Sam's smile could light up a room. He caught her staring at him and smiled. At that moment, Annie had lost her balance and one of Sam's coworkers caught her before she fell completely. How embarrassing that would have been! Annie thanked the kind gentlemen and made her way to the kitchen, where she poured herself another glass of wine. She had already lost track of how many she glasses she had. This was their night, and she wasn't about to ruin it by counting glasses of wine.

Annie spotted the young couple that used to live down the hall. They were only there a short while. They had managed to save enough money to purchase a house on the city outskirts. A small home with a yard large enough for children to play. Annie was excited for them. It made her think of the day when she would have children. *Sam and I will already have the perfect home.*

Pammi waved for Annie to come over. Annie knew right away the rumors must be true. Pammi had quite the belly bump and her face was glowing. Pammi was standing alone by the time Annie reached her. They made some small talk about the babies, not just one baby—Pammi was having twins, a boy, and a girl. Annie spent a few more minutes in conversation.

She felt bad but listening to Pammi go on and on about baby stuff wasn't something she wanted to think about or talk about this evening. They talked for a while to catch up, but Annie was distracted. Her focus was on Sam. *I don't see either one of them.* It was at that moment that Annie excused herself from the conversation. "It was great chatting with you!" said Annie. "Good luck with the babies, please send us pictures once the babies are born."

Annie's eyes scoured the room—she had lost of track of Sam. Finally, she spotted him in the kitchen, pouring a glass a wine. But it wasn't just a glass of wine for him, he was pouring one for Sally too. Annie was furious, as she watched Sally flirting with Sam. She'd made her way to the kitchen. Annie marched over to Sam. "Sam, may I speak with you in the bedroom, please?" Sally looked offended, she realized she wasn't invited to this so-called meeting. She rolled her eyes as Annie grabbed ahold of Sam's arm.

"Annie, is everything okay?"

Annie's mind raced as she struggled for something to say. She faked a look of concern. "Sam, I think we are going to run out of wine?" *Oh my god, did I just say that? This was my big concern—my need for a private meeting?* Annie didn't stray away from it, she had nothing better to come with. *A few glasses of wine and my brain has already become a little foggy.*

"Oh, Annie Jones, are you feeling a little tipsy? Your words are slurred and well, the thought that we might run out of wine is silly. We have plenty of wine for everyone, in the apartment and probably enough for everyone in the building," Sam laughed.

Annie was relieved that Sam fell for her invented crisis. Sam didn't have the slightest incline that she was doing everything in her power to keep Sally away from him. She hated to think it, but Sam was naïve. Sally was aware of that fact as well. Sally knew she could have Sam wrapped around her finger before he even realized what was happening. Annie waited for Sam to comment on Sally being there this evening. She wondered if even he noticed that Sally was flirting with him. She decided it was time to find out. "Sam, one more thing," said Annie. "Did you invite Sally here this evening, or was she a guest of ex-husband Tom's? I saw he was here earlier, but I haven't seen him since."

Sam responded hastily, Annie was sure he wanted to get back to the party. He held Annie's arm gently— trying to balance her and keep her falling on the floor.

"I don't know Annie; I don't remember inviting her, but it's possible that I ran into her somewhere and mentioned it. You know how excited I have been about this dinner party. Besides, I am sure the two of you have a lot of catching up to do, I know you were best friends in college."

Annie shrugged her shoulders. Sam was usually clueless, when it came to women, and she was sure that tonight was no different. She stood on tippy toes to kiss him. He didn't resist. Annie felt lightheaded as she moved her lips against his. His lips were soft and wet. She wanted more and she wanted it now!

"Annie Jones, as much as 1 love your willingness to continue with this, we have guests in the other room, and we are their hosts." Annie looked into Sam's eyes, making a boo lip, she let her heels fall back onto the floor, smoothed her hands over her dress and walked toward the bedroom door. Sam followed closely behind her. He was so close, she could feel his breath on her neck. Oh, how badly she wanted to turn around and make out with him some more. *It must be the wine.*

Annie looked at her watch, the time seemed be moving more slowly now than ever. Her mind was set on one thing and that was Sam. She was ready and willing to be devoured by the man she loved.

Another glass of wine seemed like the perfect idea. Annie walked into the kitchen. Sally had already moved into the living room. Annie spotted her sitting on the couch with her hand on one of Sam's coworkers' thighs. Annie was quite content to see that she had moved on.

Annie looked around for Jersey. She hadn't seen him since she and Sam had their meeting in the bedroom. She smiled when she finally discovered his whereabouts. There he was sucking up to Eileen, their neighbor. Annie guessed Eileen to be in her mid-fifties. She felt bad for the woman. her husband passed a few years ago, and since then Annie barely saw her. She was surprised to see her here tonight.

"Good boy Jersey," Annie mumbled under her breath. She felt proud as though she could somehow take credit for Jersey's compassion. She didn't hesitate to walk over there even though she was finding herself to be slightly off balance. She quickly spotted a chair and pulled it up to sit alongside Eileen and Jersey.

"Hello Eileen, I am so happy you could come tonight. Sam and I wanted to invite as many of our neighbors as we could for a chance to say goodbye."

Eileen had a confused look on her face, "Goodbye? Where are you going? Will you and Sam be leaving together? He is such a nice young man. Is he dating that woman he was talking to earlier?"

Annie's head was spinning, partly from the wine and partly from Eileen's non-stop questions.

"Oh, I am so sorry, Eileen. I just assumed everyone knew. Sam and I have a house in Murphy Texas. It was part of a sizeable inheritance from my Uncle Jack." Mentioning her Uncle Jack, immediately made Annie think of Molly. Eileen must have noticed the distressed look on Annie's face and asked, "Are you ok Annie?"

"I am so sorry Eileen; I don't know what has come over me." Eileen patted her hand, as she sat next to her.

"Why don't you pull your chair closer dear, and you can tell me about what you has so upset." Annie nodded and sat down beside her. Annie wanted to avoid sharing too much but after a few moments into the conversation, she found herself feeling better. Then suddenly, she could feel the wine churning in her stomach. *God please don't let me throw up right here.*

CHAPTER 16

Annie Locks Herself into the Bathroom

Annie excused herself and raced to the bathroom but not before Jersey snuck in. She sat on the toilet holding her head into her hands. "This wasn't how I had planned this evening to go," she said to Jersey. Jersey responded by moving even closer to her.

"It's okay Jersey, she said as she patted his back. "I just need to get ahold of myself." Within in seconds, she pushed Jersey to the side, flushed the toilet and turned out the light. Annie could feel the vomit coming to the top of her throat. She couldn't pretend it wasn't there and she heaved over and over—as she hugged the toilet. Feeling a bit of relief, she sat down beside Jersey, who was now watching her. Annie imagined that Jersey had witnessed Julee getting sick on several occasions, which is why he had such a distressed look on his face. She patted him on the head, tears still rolling down her cheeks. This was not the evening she planned or wanted. She held her head in her hands again and cried.

Suddenly, she heard a soft knock on the door. She sat as quietly as she could hoping whoever it was would go away. Then she heard it again, knock, knock, this time followed by a voice. "Annie? Are you okay? Open the door!"

"I'm fine Sam, will you please leave us alone for a few moments?" "Us," Sam asked? She couldn't help but smile. She was proud of herself at times. she could sense a little jealousy in his voice. *There is no harm in keeping him on his toes, is there?*

"Sam, it's only me and Jersey. He was kind enough to keep me company in here. Isn't that right Jersey," responded Annie.

"Annie unlock the door! I'm worried about you," Sam shouted!

Annie panicked and quickly pushed herself up from the floor before the guests overhead Sam yelling. Jersey stood up as though he was going to somehow guide her to the door. Annie rubbed his head. "I love you, Jersey. Thank you for looking after me."

As soon as Sam heard the door lock click, he bursts into the bathroom. Before Annie realized what was going on, he was whisking into her bedroom. Annie didn't fight him; she didn't have the energy. She was no more than a puddle by this time. She would have called anyone, in this condition, a sloppy drunk.

Annie laughed out loud as Sam helped her, "Sam, are you trying to take advantage of a drunk girl?" She knew, by the tone of Sam's voice, he was not trying to take advantage of her. He was angry. He didn't bother to respond to her question but sat her on the bed, as if she were a child. He proceeded to remove her high-heeled shoes and her dress. He gently eased her body back, let her head fall to the pillow and covered her. Annie could feel the covers as he placed them softly over her body and gently kissed her forehead.

"I love you Annie Jones," she heard him say as he closed the door.

"I love you too Sam, "Annie whispered. She was sleeping before she had finished her next thought.

The bright sun that was shining through the window caused Annie to wake up earlier than she had planned. She fumbled for her phone that lay on the nightstand. Everything that happened last night was a blur. *How could Sam let me sleep through the whole night?*

Annie retrieved her phone and looked at the time. She rubbed her eyes in disbelief. She couldn't remember the last time she had slept until ten o'clock. She heard the cupboard door close in the kitchen. *Sam must be making coffee. I can't go out there just yet—I am so embarrassed. His friends were probably wondering what happened to me, or even worse! Sam told them what happened to me. I was drunk, vomiting in the toilet, and he put me to bed like a child! Oh, the horror!*

Annie felt movement at the foot of her bed, she was happy to see that Jersey had spent the night with her. *I wonder if he has been outside yet. I wonder when the last time was that he was* outside. "Okay Jersey, you're such a good boy. Let me throw some clothes on and I will take you outside to go potty."

Annie grabbed some sweats and tee shirt from her dresser drawer. She dreaded the thought of not showering first. but this was an emergency. It wouldn't be fair to make Jersey wait even longer. God knows, how long it had been since he had been out last.

Jersey was now standing in front of her with his tail

wagging. She knew that she was running out of time. "Okay buddy, I promise I'm coming just let me throw my sneakers on and we can go."

Annie planned to sneak past Sam. She was too embarrassed to look at him right now. Annie followed Jersey down the hall. She expected to hear a wise remark from Sam, but what she heard was much, much worse!

CHAPTER 17

The Sleepover Guest

Annie heard a female voice before she even made it to the kitchen. "Annie, would you like a cup of coffee?" Annie could feel her heart racing. She felt sick to her stomach and was certain she was going to throw up. She knew the voice right away, it was Sally. *What is she doing here? Where is Sam? Oh my god, what happened between the two of them last night?*

Annie struggled to keep her emotions under control. She fought hard to contain the ragging lunatic within her. She did not want to lose her self-control. She gave herself a moment before she allowed herself to speak.

"Sam had to run an errand this morning, he said he would be back in about an hour." Annie didn't respond, her only reaction was to get Jersey outside as quickly as possible—for everyone's' well-being.

Annie was thankful for Jersey and his need for having to relieve himself. She was already dreading the trip back to the apartment. Her head was racing. She never should have drunk so much. *This is your* fault*! You knew Sally had her eyes on Sam and you let this whole thing happen? But wait, what thing happened? It is possible that Sally came over this morning. No, not dressed in one of Sam's button shirts. It was still possible that Sally spent the night but did not sleep in Sam's room. Yes, that was still a possibility. I need to give Sam the benefit of the doubt. I need to believe that.* She watched Jersey mull around the tiny patch of green grass. She didn't bother rushing him. T*he sun is shining, and despite how I look, being outside with Jersey was better than being inside with Sally. once more. Why Annie, why did you have to ruin the one night you were looking so forward to?*

Annie sat down on the bench and pulled out her cell-phone. She decided she was going to check on Molly and give her dad a call. These days, more than ever, Annie was missing Molly. It was nice to have met Jersey but, he was no replacement for Molly.

She dialed her parents' number. She hoped that one of them were in the house to hear the landline ring. Although they both had cellphones, they rarely used them or even bothered to carry them—especially if they were at home.

The phone rang once, Annie's dad answered—it was good to hear his cheerful voice. Annie thought it was strange that her dad was answering all her phone calls, lately. She was still in Texas the last time she could remember her mom answering the phone. "Hi Dad, is everything okay with Mom? I noticed you are the only one that ever picks up the phone when I call?"

"Hi kitten," he said. Annie smiled when she heard him say that, and she always would. "Hi dad!" replied Annie, trying to sound upbeat.

"What's wrong Kitten, you sound upset?" Annie wondered

how he could have possibly noticed. that—she did everything she could to sound as upbeat as possible.

"Oh, I am good Dad, I am just sitting on the bench outside with Jersey, waiting for him to go potty. He is such a good boy. You would love him! How is Molly, Dad? I miss her so much!"

Annie could feel the tears welling up in her eyes. She wasn't sure if it was because she missed Molly or if it was because of what she saw this morning. She was afraid to go back to the apartment. She was afraid of what Sally might tell her. Annie knew she only had herself to blame. She should have told Sally about her feelings for Sam. She should have made it a point to tell Sally to keep her hands off Sam. *This is my fault: I am the one who got drunk last night and passed* out!" Annie are you okay?" her dad asked. "You don't have to worry about Molly, she is doing fine. In fact, she is better than fine. Your Mom has become so fond of her. I am not sure she will be ready to send her home and her allergies, well they seemed to have disappeared. Yep, Annie, you heard me right. Your mom's allergies to dogs just disappeared. Molly has been sleeping in our bed since the second night." Annie heard the chuckle in her dad's voice, and she couldn't help but smile. They both often wondered about her mom's so-called allergies to dogs and Molly proved them right.

Annie laughed, "We knew it Dad, we knew it all along!"

"Molly is right here Annie, why don't you say hello to her."

Annie made some small talk with Molly. She told her how much she missed her. She told her about Jersey. She was sorry that Molly didn't get a chance to meet him. She promised her that she would bring her to New York the next time they visited. *What if Sam and Sally are a couple now? What if Sam doesn't come back to Texas with her? What if she must give up the apartment in New York?*

Annie felt sick to her stomach again and got off the phone as quickly as possible. She was afraid her dad was going to ask her more questions, and she was not prepared to answer them. She sat on the bench for a few more moments—stalling. The thought of going back to the apartment made her feel queasy. She wasn't prepared for what Sally might tell her. Annie found out a few months ago that Sally had always been interested in Sam. She knew that the feelings weren't mutual. She also knew that she had rejected Sam and worried that her performance, last night, may have ruined any future they may have had together.

Annie couldn't help but wonder if Sam's feelings had changed toward Sally. She was still as gorgeous as she had been in college. Annie found her to be much more annoying these days but that could in part that now they both wanted the same thing, Sam!

"Before we go back to the apartment, Jersey, I am going to make one more phone call." Jersey didn't bother to look up at her. He was happy wandering around sniffing every inch of the small area. She was thankful he was able to amuse himself.

She dialed Kevin's number. She needed to know how Julee was doing and when she would be coming home. She was aware of just how difficult it was going to be to say good-bye to him when—his momma did come home. It was easy to offer to take him for a few days while Julee was in the hospital, but Annie hadn't mentally prepared herself for the time she had to say goodbye. But of course, that is what she wanted because that would mean, Kevin's sister, was going home and Jersey would also be going home, his home.

Kevin didn't answer the phone right away and just as Annie was getting ready to hang up, she heard his voice. "Hi this is Kevin." She assumed he didn't recognize her phone number yet.

"Kevin, hi, this is Annie. I am glad I caught you. I was wondering how your sister was doing and if you had heard when she might be coming home?" There was a long pause followed by a whispered voice.

"Annie, I have been meaning to talk to you." Annie found those words to be puzzling. She just saw him last night.

"Annie, I know we just saw each other last night, but of course, that was not the time or place to be speaking about my sister. Besides, you looked a little, well, a little tipsy if I could be so blunt?" Kevin laughed but Annie failed to see the humor. She was embarrassed by her actions. A grown woman unable to control her alcohol was not a pretty sight.

"Kevin, what do you need to tell me about Julee?" He was being vague, and it was causing her concern.

"Kevin, you do realize that Sam and I are only in New York a few more days and that is because you asked us to look after Jersey. We extended our visit for a few more days to allow time for Julee's tests results. We don't want to see Jersey get bounced around but understand—our life is in Texas."

"I understand," said Kevin apologetically. "Can my wife and I stop by later so the four of us can talk?"

Annie agreed. She hung up the phone shaking her head. She was looking forward to leaving New York—now more than ever. It's time for Kevin and his wife to take care of Jersey themselves. Annie was angry at the world now. She was angry at Sam and Sally, she was angry at herself, and now she was angry at Kevin.

"Okay buddy, let's go face this music."

Annie slowly opened the back door. She was hoping they

could make it back to the apartment without running into anyone she knew. The lobby was surprisingly quiet. For a moment she wondered where everyone was. She looked at her watch, and realized it was a Sunday. No one was out and about yet. Most businesses weren't opened yet, so the coast was clear.

Annie's mind was racing, as she and Jersey rode the elevator. She dreaded having to confront Sally. She was certain that Sally was intentionally trying to make her jealous. Annie made up her mind to no longer avoid the situation. It was time to face whatever may or may not have happened, between Sally and Sam, last night. The elevator stopped and the door opened. There was no turning back now. "Come on Jersey!"

Annie opened the door softly. Her eyes searched the apartment. She was almost ready to let out a sigh of relief, then she heard Sally's voice calling out from the bathroom. "Sam is that you?" Annie wanted to ignore her, but she knew Sally would just keep calling out his name until she said something.

"Sally, it's me, Annie. Jersey and I are back from our walk." Annie didn't hear any response. She assumed Sally was disappointed that it was not Sam.

When Sally returned to the kitchen, it was clear that she had taken a shower. Even though her clothes were from last night's dinner party, she looked gorgeous. Her hair was freshly washed, and she even took the time to blow dry that beautiful mane of hers. Not a single hair was out of place. Even her face looked radiant. Annie was certain that Sally had helped herself to her makeup, hairdryer and perhaps even her brush Sally knew, from their college days, that Annie didn't like to share her personal stuff, and this included Sam.

"When did you say Sam would be back," Annie asked?

"Oh, Annie I am so sorry I missed you, at the party, last night. We had such a wonderful time!"

Annie didn't bother to ask who it was that had such a fun time, it certainly wasn't Annie.

With the wave of her hand, Annie tried to dismiss the whole conversation. She needed to find a new topic. She knew she would explode uncontrollably at any moment if she didn't find something else to talk about and quickly.

"Jersey, come here boy, do you want to have some lunch?"

Sally looked at Annie with a confused look on her face. "Annie, do dogs really eat lunch? I thought they only ate once or twice a day but, lunch too?" Annie smiled. Jersey never ate more than twice a day, but today she was using him for a distraction. Sally didn't need to know that. Besides, Jersey didn't mind the extra dish of food. "Just for today," Annie whispered to him.

Annie heard the doorknob click. *Thank God!* She knew it had to be Sam and she was hoping now that he returned, Sally would say her goodbyes and be on her way. *But what if she was wrong? What if something did happen between them last night? What if he walks in and kisses or even hugs Sally, what will she do then?*

CHAPTER 18

Three is Not Company

Sam walked in and tossed his cell phone on the table. He was dressed in shorts and a tank top. Annie guessed from the way he was dressed he may have gone for a jog or perhaps the gym?

"I'm going to take a quick shower and I'll see you lovely ladies in two minutes. Then we can plan our day. " *Annie* wasn't sure what exactly Sam meant by that, but she was now feeling sick to her stomach.

Sally smiled in Annie's direction. "Annie dear, may I borrow something to wear? It doesn't look like I will be headed home anytime soon. Perhaps you have a shirt dress or something simple that I could borrow— I am a few sizes smaller than you, but I can make it work." Annie was now full of rage. *First, Sally, you are not a few sizes smaller than me. You may be smaller in some areas, but I am sure we are close to the same size. Second, if you really wanted to borrow something from an old college friend, you should be more polite.*

Annie spoke with her teeth clinched, "I'll go see what I can find for you to wear Sally—feel free to help yourself to coffee or tea. Everything you need is in the kitchen." Sally didn't catch the hint and followed Annie. Jersey tagged along with a confused look.

Sally pushed past Annie. "Come on Annie, find me something sexy in this closet of yours!" Sally had a devious grin, on her face, as she spoke—the kind of look that always made Annie feel nervous and nauseous.

Annie pulled her closet door open and began moving her clothes around. *The last thing on earth I want to do right now is to find Sally something to wear, let alone something sexy.* This is cruel," Annie whispered to herself. Even Jersey seemed confused by this morning's events.

"I really like your bedroom Annie, it's small but chic." Annie was thankful that Sally had moved onto to something else and was no longer peering over her shoulder. Annie didn't respond. She was too busy looking for a mundane, paper bag-look for her dear friend Sally. Annie felt ashamed of herself. *None of this is Sally's fault. It's my fault. I could have been Sam's finance if I had accepted his proposal. I am not going to let my feelings for Sam ruin our day. We can all hang out together just like we did for years when we were in college. We spent a lot of time together, just the three of us.*

Annie searched through her closet, until she spotted a dress, way in the back. She hadn't worn it in years, and she knew she wouldn't miss it. It was a simple black dress, that Annie found to be clingy and uncomfortable. She whipped out the dress with a big smile on her face and turned to Sally. "How about this one? I know it doesn't look like much, but I am sure you will look amazing in it!" *Here you go tramp!!*

Sally turned around to face Annie. "It's perfect!" Sally smiled as Annie handed her the dress. Annie watched in horror and surprise as Sally stripped off her clothes. Annie rushed over to close the door.

"What if Sam sees you?"

Sally laughed, "Annie would that be such a horrible thing—for Sam to see me half naked? I mean, I have maintained myself all these years and I would say I have done well." She leaned forward and whispered, "I even had a boob job a few years ago! What do you think?" Annie's mind was racing—she struggled to respond. She found the whole situation extremely uncomfortable.

"Um, very nice," said Annie. Annie wondered if Sally ever considered modeling—she was that beautiful. Although Annie didn't consider herself beautiful, she knew that the opposite sex was very attracted to her. Annie would never get a boob job or any other kind of reconstructive surgery. She was content with her own beauty.

Sally slid the dress over her head and smoothed it over her hips. Twirling around in a circle, as though they were still back in their college days. "Well, what do you think," she asked? She was obviously quite happy with Annie's choice. Much to Annie's surprise, she looked amazing. Annie wondered if she should have given the dress a chance. All this time, it was just hiding away in her closet, waiting to be worn. Annie expression said it all.

"The dress looks great!" said Annie.

"I love it, Annie! I couldn't have picked a better dress myself!" Sally squealed with delight, making Annie even more irritated.

Sally walked over to Annie's closet. "Annie dear, do you

have any sandals that would go with this dress? I don't really want to wear my heels from last night."

"Sally, if you remember correctly, I wear a size seven shoe and the last I remember, you wear a size eight."

Sally nodded, "Well then heels it is!"

Annie smiled at Jersey; she knew what he was thinking, because she was thinking the same thing. *Sally is too phony and over the top for me. I have two options; I can let Sally and Sam go together alone today, or I can tag along. There was no decision, I am going no matter what.*

Sally looked at Annie sizing her up. "What about you Annie, do you want me to pick something out for you to wear?" She knew Annie very rarely dressed in a provocative way. Annie wasn't sure exactly what Sally was up to, but she made it clear she would be choosing her own outfit today.

Annie heard Sam's bedroom door open and close behind him. *He must be out of the shower. How do I keep Sally busy and out of Sam's bedroom while I get ready? Who am I right now and why am I letting her get under my skin?*

"Sally, there is this great show on Netflix, I'll turn it on for, you so you can watch it, while I take a shower."

"Sure, Annie that's fine. Jersey and I will stay right here while you shower. Unless of course Sam calls, in need of assistance."

The shower was probably the quickest Annie had ever taken. She barely took the time to dry off, before throwing on her outfit. Annie was happy with her choice. It was a one-piece short set. The top was a skimpy halter top that tied in the back, and the bottoms were short and snug fitting. The pattern was tropical— perfect for this time of year. Annie remembered the day she purchased it. She had stumbled across a sale at one of the high-end boutiques. She loved it as soon as she saw it. She knew it wasn't something she would not normally wear, but she just had to have it.

Annie slipped it on quickly and went to the mirror. She was pleased with her look and more importantly, she knew Sam was going to love it! She hauled out a pair of high heeled sandals—not to be out done by Sally. *Sam is going to love this outfit. Sally, you're not the only one who can dress to impress.*

—◆—

CHAPTER 19

Sally has an Idea

There was a knock at the door and Jersey let a loud bark. It was something he rarely did, but this morning has been eventful. Annie was turning the knob of the bedroom door when she heard Sam saying hello to someone. She crept the door open and listened. She was sure it sounded like Kevin. *I told him that he could stop by later, not later as in an hour.*

"We might as well go out there." Annie heard Sam invite him in and offer him a seat. "Hey Kevin, I wasn't expecting you until later.

Kevin went on to speak. His words left Annie in a state of disbelief. Kevin's sister Julee wasn't coming home any time soon. She would be going to a rehab center, and the probability of her getting well, anytime soon was exceedingly small.

Annie listened as Kevin explained. She saw the tears in his eyes and heard the rattle in his voice. She knew this wasn't easy for him. Annie's mind immediately went to Jersey. *Oh my god! Who is going to look after Jersey? Where will he go?* Annie didn't know how to say it, she ran a few scenarios through her mind before choosing what she thought would be the right one.

I am sorry your sister is not getting any better but what about Jersey? Did she really want to cause more stress for Kevin? We can't stay in New York any longer. Molly is waiting for me to come home, and we need to get back.

Annie stared at Kevin. Although Kevin wasn't Annie's favorite person, she could see he was in pain. He knew the prognosis for his sister wasn't good and he was not prepared to deal with it. "I don't know what I will do if something happens to her. She is the only family I have left."

Sam spoke up, "Kevin, I am so sorry man, I know you love your sister so much. I am not sure how to ask you this, but what is going to happen to Jersey?"

Kevin put his head down and spoke in a whispered voice, "Jersey will be staying at a shelter for dogs. They have a place for dogs whose owners can no longer care for them. I thank you both so much for caring for Jersey these past few days. It has meant the world to my sister, knowing that he was being well cared for.

Annie burst into tears and ran to the bathroom as fast as her legs would take her. *This is not fair! This is not fair to Julee and it's certainly not fair to Jersey!* She could hear Kevin still talking but she was afraid to listen. Like a child, she put her hands over her ears, sat in a fetal position on the floor and sobbed.

There was a knock on the bathroom door. It was Sally. "Annie honey, are you okay?" *Of course, I'm not okay! What a stupid question to ask!* "I would like to come in, if that's okay with you." Annie gently opened the door, and Sally entered the bathroom. Sally watched as Annie returned to her fetal position. She sat down beside her. "I am so sorry Annie: I know how much you love Jersey. He's a lovable guy!" She smiled and Annie could hear the sincerity in her voice. *Who is this girl?*

Annie didn't know how to respond. Here Sally, was sitting here with her, trying to cheer her up. Not more than an hour ago Annie would have given anything to see Sally walk out their apartment door and never come back.

Sally put her arms around Annie and Annie cried. She cried so hard she wasn't sure if she was ever going to be able to stop the tears.

"You know?" said Sally. "You don't necessarily have to say goodbye to Jersey!"

Annie's ears perked up. "What do you mean? Kevin has already made the arrangements at the shelter and that's what Julee wanted. If Jersey stays at the shelter, they promised Kevin that Jersey would be able to visit her occasionally."

"Sally, you just don't understand!" Annie snapped at Sally and then quickly apologized.

"Annie it's obvious to me that you love Jersey, and he should stay with you and Sam. He's happy here. You have given him a home in just a few short days, he has already adjusted."

"Sally, that's what you have forgotten. Sam and I don't live in New York anymore. I know we have the apartment for six more months, but my home is with Molly in Murphy Texas." Annie rephrased that statement. "Our home is in Murphy, Texas."

Sally's eyes grew wide, and Annie could tell by the look on her face, she had forgotten that the whole reason for the dinner party was to say goodbye to their friends and coworkers.

"Annie we can figure this out, but you have to calm down so you can think with a clear head." *Who is this girl sitting on the floor with me trying to help me figure out a way to keep Jersey? Now I remember why we were friends in college. This is sally underneath the fluff and polished exterior. This is my friend Sally!!*

"We are going to come up with a plan, Annie! we are going to come up with a good plan!"

Annie wasn't sure why or how that statement made her feel better, but it did. Two heads were better than one, right?"

A few moments later Sam knocked on the bathroom door. "Is everything okay in there?" Sally responded, as Annie regained her composure.

"We'll be out in a minute Sam. A long minute, ok?"

Sally sat on the floor coming up with numerous scenarios. Annie was surprised at how helpful Sally was being. Finally, the two had come up with an idea that they thought would work for everyone involved. Sally opened the bathroom door and they both walked out. Sally led the way and sat down on the floor, by Jersey. Annie was happy that Kevin had stayed so long.

"Kevin, I am so sorry for my outburst, but I love Jersey, we love Jersey, and we don't want to see him go to a shelter. He deserves to be with family."

Kevin didn't hesitate to jump in, "Annie, I have already told you; my wife and I cannot keep Jersey!"

At first Kevin's words infuriated Annie, *I know what he meant to say, it's not that they can't keep Jersey, it's that they won't.* But Annie knew some people just didn't have it in them.

"Kevin, please let me finish." Annie looked to Sally for reassurance. She continued to talk— barely looking at Kevin.

"I would like Jersey to come live with us in Murphy until Julee gets better."

Annie searched Sam's eyes for an approval, and she got

just what she was hoping for. Sam looked at her in a way that told her it was fine with him. She felt instantly relieved that Sam was more than okay with Annie's idea.

Kevin sat quietly, trying to process what Annie has just said.

Annie continued, "Kevin, we can bring Jersey to New York for a visit when your sister is feeling better, and in the meantime, I will be happy to share photos and videos. We can even facetime once a week—when Julee is up to it. Kevin, we have beautiful property in Murphy. We have a large field for Jersey to run, and we have a pond that is perfect for swimming. Molly and Jersey would each have a friend, while he is there. It would work out perfectly for everyone."

"Annie, I appreciate your willingness to help us out, but we aren't even sure that my sister will get better. You do understand the chances of her ever going home are slim, right?"

For some reason, Kevin wasn't sharing Annie's optimism. She thought it was a great idea. It was good for her, Sam and of course Jersey. Annie sat still for a moment—waiting for a response.

Kevin stood up and walked toward the apartment door, "I'll be in touch, let me get Julee's blessing before I make any kind of commitment. Julee loves Jersey, probably more than life itself. I must be sure that she is okay with him living in another state. Annie nodded, she understood. She loves Molly more than anything and in just a short amount of time she has come to love Jersey.

As soon as the door closed behind Kevin, she blurted out, "I am not letting him take Jersey to a shelter!" Sam walked over to Annie, putting his arms around her, he gave her one of his famous long lasting bear hugs that had always made her feel better.

"Sam he can't do this to Jersey!" Jersey, having heard his name, came walking over to them— without a care in the world. He had no idea that his world was about to change. Sally was in the kitchen making coffee. Annie felt comforted by Sally's presence. She hoped this could be a turning point in their relationship. She saw a side to Sally that she had forgotten existed. Funny how life has a way of turning everything upside down and now Sally was the least of Annie's worries.

Sam stood up and clapped his hands, "Come on ladies, we have time to figure this out, but the day is ticking away, and I want us to get out and enjoy the day!" Sally and Annie both had to laugh at that one. Sam had no idea what he was volunteering for. Sally sat her coffee cup in the sink, and they all headed towards the door.

Annie pivoted on her heels and headed back to the kitchen. "Come Jersey, come get your treat, you hold down the fort and be a good boy!" She patted his head and laughed as she watched him devour his treat. She wasn't sure where he found his appetite, but he always had one. She filled his water bowl and headed for the door. Sam closed the door behind them and out into the streets they went.

CHAPTER 20

Introduction to Isaac

The sunshine seemed to invigorate the three of them as they started the day's adventure. As they walked along, Annie thought about how much she loved her time here. The city never slept, it was always moving. The streets were alive with people making their way through their day. Annie found the food aromas to be almost intoxicating. She loved the way the city had educated her about food, and despite all the hustle and bustle, the city provided Annie with an unexpected sense of anonymity. She would miss all these things—she smiled as they walked along.

"Okay ladies, I thought we could go to visit the art gallery today." Sam said, as he searched Annie's and Sally's eyes for approval. "A friend of mine, Isaac, has a piece of art that is on display, and I told him I would do my best to be there." Sally was on board; she had a minor in art and would often take Annie on day trips to see the different artists' displays. Annie nodded in agreement.

"But first ladies, I am going to take you to the pub a few blocks from here!" said Sam.

Sally rolled her eyes, "Really Sam? The word pub just sounds so, you know pub-ish!"

Annie and Sam both laughed this time. "Come on Sally, don't you remember our college days we lived at pubs like this—food trucks and bistros too." Sally didn't respond and rolled her eyes again, she walked slowly behind them as though trying to prolong the inevitable, eating at a pub.

When they reached the building, Sam ushered them both around the corner. They sat on a lovely patio with a chic-earthy tone. There were at least ten tables with chairs and a few barstools that fit snuggly up to the outside bar. A waterfall that separated the two in a very romantic kind of way. Sam marched toward a table near the back to be away from the street. Annie and Sally followed closely behind him. "This isn't so bad, is it?" Sam asked—looking directly at Annie. Annie figured he was afraid to ask Sally's opinion, or he just didn't want to know. Sam could behave that way at times.

Annie nodded her head, "This is perfect Sam!" Sam smiled and invited them to sit with a swooping hand gesture. The wrought iron tables were small and round, with a beautiful white enamel finish. The chairs were very classic and built for comfort. The chairs pads had different boho patterns on them. Lanterns surrounded the canopy giving it an even more romantic feel. Annie wished for one second that it was just her and Sam.

The three of them walked side by side as they headed for the art gallery. It was a small gallery, but Sam was proud of Isaac, and wanted to show his support.

Sally couldn't stop asking questions about Isaac. "Sam, tell me more about your friend, Isaac. Is he married? How long have you known him? Does he live around here?"

"Sally, when we get there, you can ask him all these questions yourself. I'm sure he will be flattered to see your interest in him," Sam said sarcastically. Sally made a huff sound and they continued walking in the direction of the gallery.

"I'm sorry ladies, just a few more blocks, somehow I thought it was closer than this." Sam reached out for Annie's hand. Annie was surprised! *Was it possible that nothing happened between Sally and Sam last night? Or was Sam just being friendly.* She looked over at Sally and smiled! Sam had ahold of Sally's hand. *The Three amigos.*

. As they rounded the corner, Sam shouted out, "There it is!" It was a small building that sat only a few feet from the street. it was an older building that had been converted into an art gallery. There were marble stairs that led to the double glass door entrance and the windows were cathedral-like stained glass, which reminded Annie of her church. *I am not sure who did the renovating of this building, but they went through a lot of trouble to maintain its nostalgic look.*

Sam led the ladies to the top of the stairs and then stepped in front of them. At first, Annie found that to be odd but then understood when she saw the usher. The interior of the building was much larger than it appeared from the street. It was spacious, yet inviting, when they stepped inside. The brightly lit room with its cream-colored walls added to its elegance.

Who is Isaac and why have I never met him? Annie caught a glimpse of Sally, who was now smiling ear to ear. *Sally has been returned to her element.* Annie made eye-contact with her and smiled back. Sam took them both by the hands and led them to where his friend Isaac would be.

There were several couches displayed throughout. The positioning of the couches was no accident, most of them were placed strategically—in front of the most expensive pieces.

Sam spotted the refreshment table and pulled them along, as if they were children—being led by their parent. The table was exquisite. Annie eyeballed the food, wondering if Sam knew there was going to be a buffet. She assumed he had no idea otherwise they would have just come straight here. There was so much food; Bruschetta with three types of toppings, a cheese plate with crackers, veggie plates with dips, baba ghanoush, and ranch. There were finger sandwiches on every corner, stuffed mushrooms, and her very favorite—brownie bites. If she hadn't been so full, she would have enjoyed it much more.

Sam walked to the end of the table, there were several glasses of wine already filled and placed along the inside of the table. Sam, being the gentlemen that he always has been, handed a glass to Annie and Sally. Annie couldn't recall ever seeing Sally this happy. Sally looked extremely comfortable in her surroundings, not like Annie. She felt stiff, awkward, and out of place. If it weren't for her best friend Sam, she wouldn't be here.

Annie heard a man's voice call to Sam. She turned to look around. She could her the clicking of the man's shoes. He quickened his pace to reach them. He was taller than Annie imagined. He waved as he approached them. *Funny how one gathers images in their mind of people before ever laying eyes on them. This man coming toward them, did not resemble the man I had imagined at all.* Annie glanced over to see the expression on Sam's face. She was sure that would confirm her assumption. She saw the excitement in Sam's eyes and wondered where Sam and Isaac had met. Sam was not the type to frequent art shows.

Annie felt a tap on her shoulder and a whisper in her ear. "Is that Isaac," Sally whispered?

Annie could tell that Sally was just as captivated by this young man as she was. He was the epitome of tall, dark, and handsome.

Isaac stood at least 6' foot tall. His hair was jet black, very much resembling the color as Sally's. As he got closer Annie tried to make out the rest of his features. His look was God like, a man like you would see in an action film or on a wrestling mat.

Sam approached Isaac and went in for a quick hug. He didn't waste any time doing introductions and it was clear to Annie that Sally was more than interested in Isaac.

Annie greeted Isaac with a handshake, and he went in for a peck on her cheek—his hands were strong, and his lips were soft. *What a wonderful* combination. She could still smell his cologne, a smell that wafted into her nostrils, sandalwood, musk. *It was a smell that suited him, strong, masculine,*

Annie watched as Sally put on her best performance. If Annie hadn't known any better, she would have thought Sally was nervous. Isaac stood holding Sally's hand for the longest time. His dark eyes were bouncing about as Annie watched the two of them deep in conversation. As Annie watched the two of them, she realized they had an immediate connection. Isaac was the kind of guy that Sally was attracted to in college. *Maybe I have been wrong about Sally?* Isaac guided them through the art exhibits, acting as their personal tour guide. It was clear to Annie that he spent a lot of time in this gallery. He knew so much about individual art pieces and their creators. Sally was at Isaac's side most of the time, and why not, they had a lot in common. Was it wrong for Annie to feel relieved that her old college friend had found someone else to prey upon? Annie smiled at the thought. *Sally was most definitely sizing up Isaac, and she was coming full force, poor guy doesn't stand a chance.*

Annie scolded herself for thinking so harshly about Sally. Sally was the one to console her after she heard about Jersey and the possibility of them having to leave him in foster care. *If Sally hits on Isaac, then that means nothing happened between her and Sam last night.*

CHAPTER 21

Sally is Smitten over Isaac

Isaac and Sally led the way around the gallery. It was evident that Sally had been in this art gallery before or perhaps one like it. She walked around comparing one art piece to the other. She gave her interpretation of each piece as they viewed them.

Annie on the other hand found herself getting bored after seeing all the exhibits on the first floor. "My piece is on the second floor," said Isaac, in an excited voice. Annie had no idea there was another floor. She wondered if Sam was feeling the same way. She just wanted to see Isaac's masterpiece—then they would be able to excuse themselves and go home. Sam reached over and took Annie by the hand. He knew her so well. Annie flashed him a warm smile and squeezed his hand gently. She knew that they were on the same page and felt a bit more relaxed.

Isaac saved his exhibit for last. Annie tried to envision what his work may look like, but she didn't have much to go on, she barely knew him. Isaac had a strong, masculine, mysterious look about him. She thought he resembled a man who had a lot of hidden secrets. She wasn't sure why she had that impression of him, but her instincts told her that he was no open book.

Isaac led them to his painting and with his hands covering Sally's eyes, he whispered, "This is it! This is my masterpiece." Annie's eyes grew wide. She wasn't sure what to expect, but this wasn't it. Isaac released his makeshift blind fold from Sally's eyes and, Annie could tell, she was as surprised as Annie.

Isaac's masterpiece was of a painting of the ocean-yet it was so much more than that. He used all the right colors to capture the water, the sun, and the sky. The beach, painted off to one side, was as significant as the ocean itself. There were clear depictions of children with their pails and shovels. Their mothers were hovering in the background. Each one with a look of their own, and the same could be said of their expressions. Isaac had somehow managed to capture each person's essence. His technique forced the viewer to notice everything. The painting wasn't just visually pleasing—it was a painting that touched the depths of your soul. This was a masterpiece. It was mesmerizing and so much more than Annie had expected. *Who is this man?*

Sally reached out and touched Isaac's arm. "Your painting is magnificent!" Isaac went on to explain why the painting was significant. When he was a young boy, his parents would vacation at a house in the Cape. It was their summer retreat. As a young boy he spent a lot of his summers at the beach with his mother. His father remained in the city during the week, for work. He would visit when he could get away, for a long weekend. They all listened intently, as Isaac spoke. Annie was growing increasingly weary as the day progressed. She envisioned herself in a taxi—heading home right now. Luckily, Sam could tell that she had gone as far as she could. He waited for the perfect moment to thank Isaac for the wonderful afternoon. He complimented him again on his painting—which now had a sold sign attached to it, they exchanged final good-byes and turned to leave.

"Sally, are you coming with us," Sam asked? Annie was quite certain of the answer, but she waited for Sally to respond.

"Actually, I thought I would stay here a little longer with Isaac." Sally smiled at Isaac and gave him a wink. "That is as long as you don't mind the company?" She looked amusingly into Isaac's eyes.

"I don't mind at all, in fact, I was hoping you would stick around. I have a lot more to show you." Sally smiled seductively—she was not a shy woman. If she saw a man, she wanted, she would not hesitate to let him know.

Sam didn't bother to ask Annie if she wanted to take a cab home. He was already flagging one down when they reached the sidewalk. Annie rested her head on Sam's shoulder as they made their way home... It had been a long day and she was eager to get back to the apartment and Jersey. She nodded off. She was awoken by the taxi hitting the apartment curb. Sam handed the man a twenty as they stepped out. Annie gave him a quizzical look, "Do you always tip so well?" Sam nodded his head yes not bothering to explain himself.

They entered the apartment and were immediately greeted by Jersey. He didn't bark, he stood there looking at the two of them with his tail wagging.

"Come on Jersey," said Sam. "Your momma is tired. I'll take you out and we can have ourselves a guy chat." Jersey wagged his tail even faster when Sam reached for his leash.

"Thank you, Sam." Annie said, and flopped herself on the couch. Sam walked over to her, leaned down, and kissed her on the forehead. "Jersey and I will be back in a few, why don't get in your comfy clothes and we can watch a Netflix movie."

For the rest of the evening Sam, Annie, and Jersey cuddled, up on the couch, and watched Netflix movies. Annie tried to talk to Sam about what was going to happen to Jersey. but he shut her down.

"Tonight Annie, we are just going to enjoy the here and now. We can discuss Jersey and his fate tomorrow.

CHAPTER 22

Annie Receives a Phone Call from Joe

The next morning Annie was awoken by her phone. With her eyes barely open, she struggled to reach her phone. She recognized the number immediately. It was Joe, the veterinarian, from Murphy.

"Hi Annie!" Joe said in an excited voice. "I saw your mom the other day and she told me you were still in New York. I thought I would give you a call to make sure you are still coming back. This town needs you."

Annie was surprised by his call and not quite sure what to say. So much has changed since she came back to New York. When she left Murphy, she was still considering the possibility of a relationship with Joe, but things had become complicated between her and Sam. She wanted to focus on her relationship with Sam. She was caught off guard and was not prepared to tell him that things had changed. Instead, Annie made small talk about what was going on and when they planned to return. She felt nauseous when he asked if he could see her when they returned. Of course, she had to accept.

"I'll give you a call when we return Joe, give my regards to Florence," said Annie. She was now wide awake. Jersey was only inches from her face, wagging his tail. Unfortunately, she knew all too well what this meant. She grabbed her day-old jeans, threw on a sweatshirt, and headed toward the front door. Annie was now in the habit of leaving her crocs, on the mat by the door, for these occasions. Jersey was now pacing back and forth. Annie could only assume his bladder was going to explode if she didn't move quickly. She and Sam had slept in longer than usual this morning. So, she was sure that had a lot to do with his impatience. She moved quickly to the elevator and slipped out back. They were only there for seconds before she witnessed Jersey relieving his bladder. She was sure she saw a sigh of relief in his eyes. Annie smiled, as they returned to the apartment.

Annie knew she needed to find a way to change Julee's mind about moving Jersey to a shelter. After all, she was the owner of an Animal Sanctuary. *I am only taking on one more dog, so I don't think we need to have everything fully operational to do that.* Annie decided that she was going to pay Julee a visit later that day. Hopefully, with Sam's help, get her to agree to let Jersey stay with them—temporarily of course.

Annie was excited to share with Sam, her idea to visit Julee. She knew Sam was concerned about Jersey's welfare. Sam was standing in the kitchen preparing a cup of coffee when she and Jersey walked through the front door. "You ready for a cup of coffee?" He smiled at Annie as he slid her favorite mug into the Keurig and pressed the button. He handed Annie her cup of coffee as she sat down at the bar. "Sam, we need to discuss Jersey's fate. We can't stay in New York forever. I am anxious to get back home to Molly. I miss her so much and I am sure, by now, she feels abandoned." Sam smiled. Annie knew what he was thinking.

"Annie, we have only been gone for less than a week. I know you miss Molly, and so do I but that doesn't mean that we have to make rash decisions that we will later regret."

Annie wasn't sure where he was going with this conversation, but she was sure she wasn't going to wait to find out. *I thought he was on board with the idea of us taking Jersey to Texas to live with us.* "I can only assume this has something to do with Jersey," said Sam. He knew Annie better than she knew herself. He knew she had already fell in love with Jersey and if she had her way, she would be taking him home with them.

"Sam, I think we may be able to convince Julee to let us take Jersey back to Texas with us. After all, we do have an Animal Sanctuary and Jersey needs us."

Sam couldn't help but laugh. "Annie Jones, I love you madly, but I don't think our run-down farm hardly qualifies as an Animal Sanctuary."

"Sam, please let's just pay Julee a visit and try to sell her on the idea." Sam nodded his head in agreement. Annie's mind was already made up. She would have gone to visit Julee with or without him. "You know we can't leave it to Kevin to be Jersey's caretaker."

CHAPTER 23

Annie and Sam Visit Julee

Annie asked Sam to give his friend Kevin a call. She wanted to set up a visit for this afternoon. She paced the floor while the conversation seemed to last forever When Sam ended the call. Annie shouted at him, "Well, did he say yes?" Sam hesitated, then told Annie that Kevin said he would give his sister a call and get back to us. Julee was still very weak, and they tried to keep visitors to a minimum, "Please don't get your hopes up Annie, she may say no," Sam explained. Annie knew if she could just talk to Julee she may change her mind.

Within moments, Sam's phone rang. It was Kevin. He confirmed their visit for the afternoon. He said their visit would be limited to one hour and they would be required to wear a mask—due to her weakened immune system. Sam knew Annie would do anything that had to be done to have a visit with Jersey's mom.

"I am going to take a quick shower," Annie shouted as she

ran down the hall. "We can run a few errands before it's time for the visit, also Sam we need to come up with some valid reasons that Jersey should come home with us, more than just because we want him to."

Sam yelled out sarcastically, "Who is this *we*, you are referring to, this is your idea." Annie heard him chuckle after he said it, so she he was on board.

She found herself nervous to meet Julee, sure she had spoken with her a few times over the phone, but she had never met her. Annie wasn't sure what to expect, so she tried to prepare herself for anything. Sam was grabbing Jersey a treat, as he waited for Annie to make her way down hall. Jersey was already spoiled and based on the number of snacks he has gone through in just a short time, he was sure he gained at least a few pounds.

Sam hailed down a cab when they reached the sidewalk. "I have a few errands to run before we visit the hospital. Sam, is it possible that we can stop off a few blocks ahead? I can go to the bank, the drugstore and then we can walk from there?" Sam nodded in agreement. Annie loved that about him, he was always so agreeable.

It was a quick cab ride. When they were finished, with Annie's errands, they began walking toward the hospital. Annie tried to imagine what Julee might look like. *Did she resemble her brother Kevin? Was she going to appear weak and sick? She was fighting for her life. She might be getting better, but was she up to having an in-depth conversation about whether Jersey should be allowed to move to a different state, or not? Whatever you say, do not use the word move! It sounds too permanent!*

Sam and Annie arrived at the hospital ahead of time. It was a lot smaller than they had expected. They walked toward the front of the building. It had double doors with a small alcove between them. "I suppose we could wait in here if we must," said Annie.

"Let's go inside and see what they have to say." Sam said, in his take charge voice. Annie was happy to oblige.

The young woman looked at Sam, admiringly, and Annie noticed. Sam was handsome guy he was known to turn a few heads. Annie smiled at the thought, *Sam is so naïve, he would never notice a girl flirting with him.*

Sam did all the talking while Annie stood there looking around. It had the appearance of a hospital of some sort, but she assumed it was a private one and by all appearances, an expensive one.

The young woman took down their information and waved them to the seating area across from the reception area. It was a small area but rather than the usual hard waiting chairs, that were the typical in waiting rooms, this waiting room had a few couches and a recliner. The television was perched on an arm hanger that could be moved at every angle. There were several magazines placed sporadically on the end tables. Annie didn't bother to pick out a magazine, she was more interested in getting to see Julee.

A few moments went by and the young woman from the reception area walked over to greet them. "Miss Julee will see you now." She handed them two masks and gave them a list of rules that must be adhered to. Sam and Annie both nodded their heads and listened. Annie's stomach was in knots. She was afraid of what she might see, how Julee was going to react and even worse what if she said no to Jersey coming to live with them?

When they reached Julee's room, the door was closed. They waited while the young woman, with her ponytail swinging in the air, knocked on Julee's door. Annie and Sam followed behind her. It was a typical single occupancy room. There was a TV mounted on the wall and few chairs. Julee was seated in one of the chairs and didn't seem to notice them, at first. She looked weak, tired, and frail. Annie gave her a soft smile as she worked up the courage to ask her the unthinkable. Annie doubted herself for a moment, but reminded herself, she was doing what was best for Jersey.

Julee waved her hand for them to sit down. Annie sat in the chair positioned across from Julee. She assumed the chair hadn't been moved since the last visitor because it was pulled away from the wall and faced at an angle. Annie cleared her throat and made some small talk about the weather.

"How is my Jersey boy," Julee asked? Annie could see the tears welling up in Julee's eyes. "I miss him so much, thank you for doing this. I feel so terrible, he has no idea where I am. He doesn't understand why he has been abandoned. He doesn't know why he's been left with strangers."

Annie knelt in front of Julee's chair and held her hand as she spoke. "Julee, I offered to bring Jersey into our home, in fact, I insisted on it. He is a lovely boy, and I can tell from his gentle and happy-go-lucky way that he was well cared for. Julee's head hung forward—making it impossible for Annie to see her facial expressions. Annie pulled her phone out and began showing her some photos. He had the biggest smile. It was impossible for Julee not to see that he was happy. Julee could see that he was in a warm, loving home. She held the phone in her hands, as she scrolled through the photos. Annie could see the tears rolling down her cheeks.

"I miss him you know. My Jersey has been with me since he was a puppy. I am not married and it's just the two of us. He was supposed to spend his entire life with me now here I am sitting in a hospital room waiting to die."

Annie was not prepared for that. "Julee, you're not going to die. The doctors said you are getting better. You will go home one day, and Jersey will be waiting for you."

"When are you and Sam going back to Texas," asked Julee?

"Has Kevin found Jersey a place to stay yet? He promised me that Jersey will live in a place that will bring him here to visit at least once a week. The nurses have already agreed to let Jersey visit as early as next week if all goes well." Annie smiled. *I am not sure a place like that even exists. It wasn't often that dogs in foster care were able to visit with their owners.*

"It's a shame that you are headed back home soon, looking at your photos, Jersey looks happy," said Julee.

"Julee? There is something Sam and I would like to run by you." Annie looked at Sam as she was finishing her sentence. He didn't respond, he just stared straight ahead as though she had never mentioned his name. Julee lifted her head and looked at Annie with curiosity in her eyes.

"We love Jersey. We have a large yard, back home, and our little Puggle girl Molly who is waiting for us to return. How would you feel about us bringing Jersey back home with us until you are better? It is an Animal Sanctuary after all. Jersey will love it! As you may already know Julee, we live in Texas. My Uncle left me the Animal Sanctuary when he passed. It is a beautiful farmhouse that Sam has worked tirelessly on—making improvements. It's a work in progress. Look, there is certainly plenty of room for Jersey. He will love the large fenced in yard and the pond down back—where we can go swimming—when it gets too hot. Molly loves it there and will be a perfect playmate for him."

Annie searched Julee's face—looking for a reaction. Julee looked Annie in the eyes and smiled. Julee hadn't even spoke yet, but Annie couldn't tell if that was a yes or a no.

Then Annie panicked and blurted out, "We can bring Jersey to visit once a month if you would like." Sam's head spun around, his eyes were wide open, and his stare told Annie everything he wasn't saying. She could hardly believe she said it herself—desperate times called for desperate measures. She couldn't take the risk of Julee saying no. She wondered what she would have said if it had been Molly. She wondered if she would allow strangers to take her indefinitely. Annie knew the answer to that question and that is why she said what she did.

Julee's eyes lit up upon hearing those words. "Really, you would do that for me, but you don't even know me. Besides, it would be much too expensive." Sam was trying to put in his two cents, but Annie glared at him. Luckily, Sam was easily persuaded, and he sat down.

Annie took ahold of Julee's hands. It made her heart ache to see a woman who loved her Puggle so much and not be able to care for him. Annie knew her life would be empty without Molly in it. She shuddered at the thought.

Julee smiled, and in between coughs, she thanked Annie and Sam. "I don't know how I could ever repay you," she cried. "I love Jersey more than anything in the world. He has been my companion for years. We eat together, watch TV together, and sleep together. We have never been apart." By this time Julee wasn't the only one with tears in her eyes. The situation sucked, it sucked for everyone involved, including Jersey.

Apparently, Annie didn't know the right time to shut up. "Julee, I know you said Jersey was going to be able to visit you next week. Well, what if we stayed a few more days and brought

Jersey to visit with you before we left." *Oh my god, what did I just say? What was I thinking? Oh my god, what about Molly? What will my dad say? We have already been here too long.*

Annie shot Sam a quick look and turned away. She saw the disapproval in his expression. She knew she was going to get a lecture the minute they stepped out of the hospital room.

Julee reached out for Annie and gave her a hug. Annie could see how weak she was and how this visit was taking its toll. Annie wasn't sure if it was because of the conversation or, just the visit itself that exhausted her. Annie wanted her to know that she was there for her, and for Jersey.

There was a knock on the door and Sam went to answer it. It was the head nurse telling them visitation hours were over. Annie grabbed Julee by the hands. "Everything is going to be okay," Julee nodded her head in agreement. Annie could see the fear in Julee's eyes and reassured her.

The nurse ushered them down hall, to the front door. "She is going to be okay, isn't she," Annie asked?

"Only time will tell. But I did overhear her when she mentioned Jersey coming to visit next week. If anyone or anything can help Julee get better, it's Jersey! She loves him so much. I feel like I know him already listening to her speak about him. She keeps a picture of him under her pillow." Annie had to turn away, as much she loved Jersey and wanted him to remain with them, she knew he belonged with his momma!

"We can pray!" said Annie, wiping the tears from her cheeks.

Sam opened the door. He was quiet as they walked back down the path, past the parking lot and toward the street. Annie was waiting for the lecture—the scolding, she knew she probably had coming. She knew she had no right to speak for

Sam. Annie was certain that Sam was as eager to get back to Texas. They both had become accustomed to the large yard, the quiet street, and Molly. As they reached the end of the path, Sam reached out and took Annie's hand, gently squeezing it. He didn't have to say a word. His gesture told Annie everything she needed to know. Sam was not going to lecture her about the last-minute decision she made without his approval. He felt as helpless and heartbroken as she did. "We can make this work, Annie," Sam whispered. The walk back to the main street was quiet. There was no more talk of Jersey, Julee, or Molly. Annie would occasionally lean her head in on Sam's arm as they walked. "This day has been exhausting," said Annie.

Sam agreed. "Let's grab a cab back to the apartment!"

That night they spent sitting on the couch binge watching one of Annie's favorite shows. Jersey snuggled up between them without a care in the world. Annie was excited to tell Jersey how he would get to see his momma next week. She was sure he understood what she meant. He tilted his head with his big brown eyes and gave her a smile that told her so. She wasn't going to tell Sam that she thought Jersey knew what she was saying, but Annie knew, and that was all that mattered.

Annie decided to wait to give her parents a call. Her parents loved having Molly and that they wouldn't mind taking care of her a little longer. This helped to ease her guilt for taking so long.

The next morning, Annie dialed her parent's number. This time her mother answered.? "Hi Mom, it's Annie. I have some bad news." She went on to tell the whole story making sure to leave nothing out. Annie was surprised at her mother's calming reaction.

"Okay dear, give us a call when you get back." As relieved as Annie was, she couldn't help but think of how weird the conversation had been.

The next few days flew by quickly. Annie had taken some time off, to catch up a little, and pay a visit to the office—while they were still in New York. She could bring Jersey in for her coworkers to meet. She remembered how much they loved it when she would bring Molly in for a visit.

Sam kept busy doing his own thing. His work had been piling up since they came back to the city. Annie had made the proposal to fly back home after Julee's visit with Jersey rather than drive like they had originally planned. Annie was relieved when Sam agreed. She began making all the arrangements. The plan was to fly the morning after Julee's visit with Jersey. Annie was excited at the thought of going home and even more so since they were bringing Jersey with them.

CHAPTER 24

Jersey Visits His Momma

The day finally arrived. It was time for Jersey to meet with his momma. Annie wondered if he felt lonely or abandoned. She had to dismiss those thoughts from her mind, it made her heart hurt. "Annie, today is a good day, don't ruin it by thinking bad thoughts." She mumbled under her breath.

Annie gave Jersey's fur a quick brush and threw on his sweater. There was still a chill in the air. He didn't have the sort of wardrobe that Molly had, but he did have a few sweaters, and a raincoat.

When they got to the street, Jersey behaved more excitedly than normal. Annie wondered if he had a sense of where they might be going. She was looking forward to seeing the look on his face when he sees Julee. They took the shortest route possible. Visiting schedules were limited and they were lucky to secure a time, on such short notice. They were given clear instructions to not be late, not to come inside, and limit the visit to half an hour. They were to meet Julee in the Gazebo—weather permitting, of course. Luckily, there was not a cloud in the sky.

Jersey had set the pace, and he moved quickly through the small crowds and down the streets. When they reached the hospital parking lot, He had picked up his pace. Annie released the leash, and he took off, toward the Gazebo. He moved quickly up the stairs—to greet Julee. Julee's smile seemed to light up the world. For a few moments she no longer resembled the woman they saw a few days ago. She resembled the woman she was, the woman she used to be—long before she was diagnosed with cancer, long before the cancer stripped her of everything she loved, long before it stripped her of her best friend—Jersey. Annie wiped the tears from eyes. She was determined to take many pictures of Jersey and Julee together. Annie planned to create a photo album for Julee as soon as she had them printed.

The half hour went by way too fast. Annie watched Jersey as he soaked up all the loving from his momma, that he could. Annie knew he was no dummy. He knew his momma was sick and he has probably known it for a long time. People don't give animals enough credit. They may not be able to speak but they certainly know how to communicate. They have a much better sense of non- verbal communication than human beings, and their sense of smell is off the charts. Annie snapped a few more pictures, she wanted to have several options. Julee's face showed Annie all she needed to see. She knew bringing Jersey back every month was not only the right thing to do, but it was necessary, for Julee's recovery. Annie was lost in her thoughts when a woman's voice interrupted them. "So, you must be Jersey?" Annie heard the red-headed woman say. Annie remembered her, from the first visit. Annie assumed she was the nurse assigned to care for Julee. Jersey's tail wagged as the woman walked toward him.

Julee was so proud of her boy Jersey. She held Jersey as she introduced them. "Peggy, this is my best friend Jersey." Jersey's tail wagged and his smile was incredibly heart-warming. Annie had witnessed Jersey's smile before but never as much as today. She looked at Sam, who was as teary-eyed as she was. Even with the tears in his eyes—his smile lifted the mood. Annie knew that Sam was just as thankful they decided to do this, as she was. *This poor woman has been through hell and back. She deserved a day like today. She deserved to see her best friend and longtime companion. Jersey deserved to see his momma—to kiss her and let her know that he has not forgotten her, and that he loves her unconditionally. Life is so unfair.*

Peggy sat on the bench next to Julee. She sat there silently listening to Julee reminisce about the stories of her and Jersey. *They were some great stories.*

Annie glanced at her phone to get a look at the time. Peggy didn't seem to care about enforcing the visitation rules. The sun was now shining and was getting hot. Luckily, Peggy had brought a few bottles of water with her when she came out to join them. She even brought one for Jersey, which Annie was thankful for since she hadn't given it any thought. *Peggy is a wonderful Nurse and friend; Julee was lucky to have such a wonderful Nurse taking care of her.*

It wasn't long after Annie had looked at her phone that she saw Peggy stand up. Julee's smile seemed to fade. Julee wrapped her arms around Jersey one more time. Annie watched her hug him—she was sure she was going to break him in two. Jersey didn't flinch. He kissed her all over her face. Annie had to smile; you would have thought Julee's face was smothered in peanut butter. She laughed a little, as she cried. The last thing she wanted to do today was cry, but the tears just came, one after the other.

Peggy helped Julee to her feet and held her in a standing position as she said goodbye to Sam and Annie—thanking them again for their help. "I don't know how to begin to thank you both for bringing Jersey here today. He is my family, my child, and his being here has given me strength. It has motivated me to get better so, I can be with Jersey once again."

Annie walked over to hug her, and Sam joined them. "It was our pleasure. We are here for you and Jersey. If there is anything we can do to help you and Jersey, we are here for you. We want you to get better so you two can be together." They exchanged phone numbers, emails. Annie gave her the addresses to both their New York apartment and the sanctuary.

They stood and watched as Peggy led Julee back to the hospital. Julee turned around, waved, and blew a kiss, before disappearing behind the double doors. Annie's heart sank. This had been such an emotional day for everyone. She made a mental note of everything she wanted to do for Julee. She glanced down at him. He was still smiling, and that was a good thing. He had a great afternoon with his momma, and he looked at peace.

The walk home took a lot longer than the walk to the hospital. It was clear their visit had taken its toll on them, even Jersey moved at a much slower pace. Annie was sure he was tired from all the attention he received. The sun was hot and there was very little breeze. A few more blocks and they would reach the apartment. Annie was grateful they lived in an apartment building that had central air.

When they reached the apartment, Annie filled Jersey's water bowl and gave him a small snack. He was such a good boy today, he earned it. She began to reorganize her to do list. She planned to start working on it as soon as she had uploaded the pictures from today and placed an order. *Technology is a wonderful thing.*

There were so many great photos! Annie sent Julee a text message with a few of her favorites. She was surprised when she didn't hear right back from her. Annie had to remind herself that Julee was still weak and although she put on a great front this afternoon, she was sure it took its toll.

Since they were flying out the next morning, Annie wandered around the apartment checking to be sure she had packed everything on their list, anything she could pack ahead of time. They didn't need to pack too much since they are keeping the apartment. But she would still need her clothes, shoes, and any papers they may need back in Murphy. Sam was stretched out on the couch watching a baseball game, that he didn't seem to be interested in. Annie didn't follow sports, so she had no idea who was playing or what game it was. He didn't seem to be interested himself, so, she assumed it wasn't one of his teams playing. She had sat with him when one of his teams were in the game and it was intense.

"Sam, are you all packed for tomorrow? We leave early in the morning," said Annie. She wanted to pack as much as she could tonight to avoid the morning rush, that always seems to ruin the mood for the entire day. She looked around the room, her suitcases were already packed and standing up by the dresser. She chose to leave some stuff behind since they would be returning in a month.

Annie was in her closet looking for her hiking boots. She

thought it would be fun to go exploring with Jersey and Molly when they returned home. As she searched the back of her closet, she heard her phone ding. At first, she was going to ignore it, but then she thought about her parents, Julee, and Molly. She didn't want to take a chance ignoring it in case there was an emergency.

It was a message from Julee. Judging from the attached message and emojis she sent, she must be in good spirits.

"You and Sam are my earth Angels, I may never be able to repay you, but you should know, I am forever grateful."

Annie smiled; she didn't feel sad anymore. She was happy that she and Sam were able to bring an afternoon of happiness, to a woman who really needed one. Annie was hopeful that the visit would help Julee find the strength and courage she needed. She responded with a short message and a heart emoji. It was getting late, and she thought Julee should rest. Annie sent her a picture of Jersey laying on the floor and a kissy face emoji and wished her a goodnight.

Annie returned to her closet and continued her search for the hiking boots. Finally, she spotted a box tucked, away on the corner-shelf, and pulled it down. She tried them to make sure they still fit. She stood up and walked around her room. She wiggled her toes to make sure there was enough room inside the shoe.

Annie heard a knock on her bedroom door, "Come on in Sam, I was just getting ready to give my parents a call and let them know what time we would be home tomorrow. I am so excited to see Molly, Sam!" Annie kicked the hiking boots off from her feet and stretched out onto the bed. "Jersey, come!" she shouted. Within seconds of calling his name, Jersey was on the bed and licking her face. Annie laughed and patted the bed for him to lie down. Sam scooched in by Annie and stretched his body out onto her bed. There was nothing uncomfortable about the two of them sharing moments in her bed, it is something they have done for years. Annie grabbed her phone and dialed up her parent's number. The phone rang and rang but no answer. Annie left them a voicemail to give her a call back. "I'll just stay with you until one of them calls." said Sam—in a semi worried voice. He knew it was unusual for one of them not to answer.

Annie clicked on the television, the three of them stretched out on the bed as they waited for her parents to return her call. Annie handed Sam the remote but when he declined, she flipped through the channels mindlessly, she was too distracted and worried to pay any attention to what was on the TV. She was still scrolling through the channels when her cell phone rang. She and Sam looked at one another and held their breath. It was her parent's phone number. Annie answered the phone hesitantly and heard her father's voice on the other end, she put the phone on speaker so Sam could hear the conversation. "Is everything okay, Dad, you sound out of breath? Sam is here and we were both worried when you didn't answer the phone?"

"Everything is fine, Annie. Your mother and I were just giving Molly a bath before you came to pick her up tomorrow. We know you are going to be busy with the two of them so we thought we would help where we could. We look forward to seeing the three of you tomorrow. We have been trying to prepare Molly for her new brother, but she doesn't pay much attention," chuckled Ben.

"Okay Dad, we are going to hang up then and let you get back to Molly's bath. I am sure Mom has her hands full doing it alone." Annie smiled as she hung up the phone.

"You are going to have a busy day tomorrow, Jersey. You are going to meet Molly, my parents and probably my brother, Brian."

Sam was still stretched out next to Annie. She could feel the heat escaping his body and running along the side of hers. He smelled amazing. For a half of a second, she considered rolling over, taking his head into her hands, and kissing his lips in a way that he had never been kissed before. But then She thought about what would happen next. *It has been a long day; I don't think I want to start something I can't finish. Things have been going so well, it's best to leave it that way, at least for tonight.* She glanced over at Sam. His arms were stretched out above his head, his eyes looked droopy, like he was going to fall asleep at any second. It was only a matter of a few minutes, Sam let out a loud yawn, leaned over, kissing Annie on the forehead, and said goodnight. *I guess I could read his mind, laughed Annie. I am so thankful that I didn't try anything silly.*

Annie's phone alarm was set for six a.m. she clicked off the television and found herself a comfortable soft pillow. Jersey curled up against her and before long they were both sound asleep.

CHAPTER 25

Returning Home

The next morning, Annie woke to the sound of the alarm buzzing. She got up immediately and took Jersey out. The rest of the morning unfolded perfectly. They were all packed and arrived at the airport in plenty of time to make the flight. Jersey was handed off to an airline associate who took care of the four-legged passengers... Annie was relieved to see that this time it was a male associate, and not Kristina. Annie didn't need that annoyance: today. They kissed Jersey on the forehead and watched the associate take him away. He didn't seem to mind. Annie was thankful they chose a direct flight.

Their flight was uneventful, and they were quickly reunited with Jersey. The Texas sun was already blazing. Annie was certain it was going to be a sweltering day. "I'll go and grab our bags Annie if you want to get Jersey?" Annie took the claim ticket to get Jersey while Sam went for the to the luggage. Annie stood in line with her claim ticket. A young woman greeted her, took her ticket, and said, "I'll be right back." A few moments later she came from a back room with Jersey. He looked tired but happy, as he wagged his tail. She bent down and gave a big kiss and hug. Annie decided to stand off to the side and wait for Sam. It wasn't long and before Sam arrived with bags. They made their way to the truck, and Sam loaded the luggage. Jersey sat between them as they made their way home... Annie was excited to see Molly's face when she sees not only them but Jersey. *It was hard to guess how Molly would feel about it all. She was used to being the princess!*

Annie's Mom and Dad were standing on their porch when they arrived. It was a nice of them to meet Annie and Sam at their house. The two of them already being there saved them a lot of extra running around, later. Sam wheeled the truck into the driveway and Annie snapped on Jersey's leash and jumped out. She raced to front porch and reached for Molly. It was the best moment ever. Molly's tail was wagging as fast as it could, and her big smile melted Annie's heart.

Molly's smile was short lived when she caught a glimpse of Jersey. She immediately looked down at Jersey and started barking. Molly continued to bark while Jersey took it in stride. He sat there with his head cocked, as Annie tried to settle Molly down. Annie could only assume he had been around dogs before either that or he was that good natured, that he didn't care. He didn't see Molly as a threat. Annie knelt on one knee, with Molly still in her arms, and reached down to pet Jersey. She whispered in Molly's ear. "Baby girl, this is Jersey. His momma is sick, and he is going to stay with us until she is better." Jersey moved in a little closer to sniff Molly. He licked her on her face just once and stood back. Molly didn't respond. The good news was that she didn't bark or growl either. Annie did this a few more times, while whispering in Molly's ear. She had to reassure her that this dog was no threat to anyone standing there, including herself. Eventually Molly seemed to warm up and Annie sat her on the ground. They all laughed as they watched Jersey and Molly circle around each other—sniffing one another. "We could go in the house, and the two of you could do this out back?" She was happy the two of them were getting to know each other and that the introduction was going well.

Annie's dad helped Sam grab the luggage from the truck while Annie and her mom went inside. Annie smiled when she looked around, it seemed like they had been away from home and Molly for an eternity. Annie ushered Molly and Jersey to the back door.

She was glad she had fenced in yard. She opened the screened door, and out they want. She watched them through the window, for a few more minutes, to be sure there wouldn't be any fighting. Annie looked at her mom, who had just sat down, and waved for her to come look out the window with her. Molly and Jersey were standing side by side—looking through the fence. "Puggle Butts," laughed Annie. She quickly snapped a photo of the two of them and sent it to Julee. Julee had asked Annie to send her a photo when they got back home. She wanted her to see how Jersey had gotten along with Molly. This photo was sure to make Julee smile.

"Oh Annie, it's so good to have you home. I hope this situation works out for the best." Annie nodded in agreement, even though she wasn't sure what her mother meant.

Annie's Mom sat back down at the table; Annie joined her. They had so much catching up to do. Each of them took their turn sharing the past week's events. Of course, Annie's mom couldn't wait to ask the question, "Annie, how are you and Sam doing? I know there were problems between the two of you before you left. Hopefully, that has been resolved."

Annie surprised her mother, "Mom, I love Sam! If he were to propose again to me today, I would most definitely say yes."

Annie's mother put her hands to heart and with a smile said, "Those words are music to my ears, dear. Does Sam know how you feel?"

Annie wiggled in her chair trying to buy herself some more time. Her mother's question caught her off-guard, for some reason. "Not exactly," she managed to say. As Annie racked her brain for something more to say. Just then, she heard the front door close and the sound of Sam and Ben's voice. Annie let out a sigh of relief. *Just in time.*

It was already nearing afternoon, Annie could hardly believe the day was going by so fast. Jersey and Molly were cuddled up together. "Look Sam!" Annie pointed to Molly and Jersey. "Look how adorable they are, I think they like each other." Sam smiled; he was thankful the transition has gone well. Annie popped up from the table and began snapping pictures with her phone. She planned to send them to Julee: later. Annie's mom was full of surprises. She heard Sam mention that he was getting hungry. Rose smiled, "I was hoping someone would say they were hungry. Ben and I prepared a dish of lasagna plenty big enough for the four of us. So, I guess you could say we have invited ourselves to dinner," Rose laughed.

"You are the best, Mom!" said Sam. He walked toward Annie's mom, to give her hug, and take the pan from Rose's hands. Sam let his hands fall when he had the pan in his hands, jokingly said "Were you expecting us to return with an army? We weren't gone long enough to give you any grand-children—well besides Jersey!" Annie's mom laughed as she looked over at Annie. Annie looked away. The conversation was beginning to get weird, and she didn't want any part of it.

Sam placed the lasagna in the oven. "Sam why don't you grab some glasses and pour us some wine," suggested Annie's Mom. "We can sit on the deck until it's time to eat." Sam nodded his head in agreement. He grabbed the glasses from cupboard and poured them a glass of Pinot Grigio. *If there was anything Sam was an expert on, it was his wine.*

"This is the best wine to pair with Italian food. We have two bottles so feel free to have as many glasses as you like." Sam said, as he smiled and lifted his glass for a toast. "Here's to us, for returning home safely. Cheers to Rose and Ben for taking such loving care of our sweet baby girl. And a toast to Jersey and Molly for filling our hearts with love and finally, to my best friend, my confidant, my girl. I love you, Annie Jones. If it takes me the rest of my life to prove that to you then so be it." Annie walked over to Sam, standing on her tippy toes she gave him a kiss. It was a long inviting kiss. A kiss that told him everything he needed to know. Annie tried to send Sam a message.

"Well now, that kiss will go down in my book as the top three!" They all laughed. *Sam was clever, there was no doubt.*

The conversations rapidly changed from one topic to the next. Annie tried to stay focused, but she was still thinking about Sam's speech, their kiss. She wanted one special evening where she could tell him everything she had been thinking, since his proposal. She wanted to tell him she loved him. She wanted to convey the message loud and clear without it being awkward. *Why did it always feel awkward?*

Rose was aware of Annie's drifting in and out of the conversations. One minute she was there and the next minute she was in her own world. "Annie dear, are you okay? Your father was speaking to you, I can only assume that you didn't hear him?"

Annie shook her head, "I'm so sorry Dad, I guess I was lost in my own world" Ben laughed, he never was the sensitive type. Annie was his little girl, his princess. He would never accuse her of being anything but polite.

———◆———

CHAPTER 26

Annie Divulges Her Secret

hile they were sitting around the table, Annie heard her phone ring. "Excuse me," she said. She ran into the kitchen to grab it from the counter. Annie looked at the number. It was, Aleena. Annie and Aleena worked on the same floor. They would sometimes to get together for lunch or after work drink when Annie was in the New York office. "Hey girl," Annie yelled! She was excited to hear Aleena's voice on the other end. Aleena was Annie's favorite coworker. She was in her mid-twenties and enjoying the life of a professional-single woman. She never had a problem with dating, in fact, men sought her out. At least that's what Annie had witnessed whenever they would go out for lunch—even more for an after -dinner drink. Aleena was taller than average, Annie guessed her to be at least five foot eight inches. She was often taller than most of the men she dated. She was the "girl next door" according to most of the men in the office her. She was kind, funny and had a love for the outdoors and nature.

Which, Annie could only assume, made her even more desirable to men. Aleena was a beautiful young woman. She had long beautiful chestnut brown hair and dark eyes to match. She didn't rely on makeup or fancy clothes. She was a natural beauty.

Aleena was known for her temper. At times she would display sudden outbursts without thinking twice. There were times when Annie had been in the office, she could hear Aleena screaming at the interns. It was shocking to see. Annie knew it was best to leave her alone and she would calm down on her own at some point during the day.

Annie wanted nothing more than to chat with her and promised to call her as soon as her parents left. Which, secretly, Annie was hoping would be soon. Annie ended the call and headed back to the porch where everyone was still gathered. She could tell by her father's movements he was getting antsy, and he would want to leave soon. "Rose, I think it's time we call it a night." Annie's Mom didn't respond, she just grabbed her purse and walked toward the screen door. Molly and Jersey darted in front of them and waited patiently.

Annie's mom laughed, "Molly dear, you need to back up so Grandma can open the door." Annie couldn't help but to smile. *Who ever thought my mom would refer to herself as Grandma, to a dog?* Sam and Annie walked them to the door, waving goodbye as they pulled out of the driveway. "Who was on the phone earlier," Sam inquired? Annie assumed he thought it was Joe, which explained why his tone sounded so inquisitory. Sam had never been the jealous type until Joe came into the picture. As much as Annie wanted to tease him, she decided not to. "It was my friend Aleena, I told her I would call her back when Mom and Dad left. Sam smiled. "You go ahead and call Aleena, the three of us will stay down here and clean up the mess."

Annie shouted behind her as she ran up the stairs, "Thanks guys!" The day had been a long one. She looked forward to kicking off her shoes and stretching out.

"Oh, how I have missed you bed!" She plopped down on the comforter and smiled. She dialed up Aleena's number and waited for an answer. Within seconds Aleena was on the other end chatting about her life as a single woman. Annie listened intently. Although she was happy that Aleena was living out her dream, Annie had chosen a different lifestyle. Annie liked romantic evenings on the couch watching NETFLIX, and long walks on the beach. Aleena was more into camping, hiking steep mountains and traveling. When it was Annie's turn to share the news of her life, she rattled on—nonstop. The one thing Annie loved about Aleena was that not only was she a great conversationalist—she was an even better listener. Annie went on to the tell the story of Jersey, his mom who had cancer, the possibility of Jersey's mom not getting any better, the possibility of her dying, and what would become of Jersey.

Annie chose to share with Aleena her desire to be more than Sam's best friend.

"Are you kidding me?" Aleena shouted. "Annie, are you kidding me? You know this is a terrible idea, right? Sam is your best friend. You two have been friends forever. If you choose to move into new territory who knows what could happen. You could wind up hating him or worse, him hating you!" Annie was shocked by what she was hearing. This is not at all what she expected to hear from her. Annie tried to defend herself and the possible-future relationship.

Aleena scolded her again. "Annie, listen to me, I am your

friend, but this is a terrible idea! Do me a favor at least wait another six months—even better, a year. You have had so many things happen between the two of you. You have moved to a different state, you bought a house, and you have not one dog, but two dogs. Annie please, please listen to your friend. I know what I am talking about." Annie didn't respond. She felt disappointed and confused. She quickly ended the call. She laid there stunned. *Was Aleena, right? Was it dangerous for us to become romantic risking our friendship? What if didn't work out, would Sam move back to New York leaving me here to tend to the Sanctuary by myself?*

That day must have taken its toll on Annie. She woke in the morning with the same clothes she had on the previous day. She searched the room for Jersey and Molly, but they weren't there. She moved to the edge of her bed, searching for her slippers, with her toes. Annie opened the bedroom door and looked around the upstairs hallway. She thought for sure, Molly and Jersey would have been waiting outside, but they were not there. She looked over to the door that led into Sam's room. She had no choice but to open his door to look for the dogs. She tiptoed to the door and quietly opened it and peeked inside. Annie smiled when she saw the three of them sprawled out. Molly was positioned on the opposite pillow while Jersey sprawled out between the two of them. Annie had to resist the urge she had of jumping into the mix of it all. She stood there admiring him. Annie had to laugh, stop being a peeping Tom, she said, under her breath. She quickly and quietly closed the door and tiptoed down the stairs into the kitchen.

Annie turned on the Keurig and grabbed a mug She stared out the window, admiring the big fenced-in yard, the fields that surrounded it, and the pond. Annie loved the pond. She looked forward to taking Jersey and Molly there soon. Annie heard the patter of paws running down the stairs. She had to laugh; she was sure they were trying to outrun each other. Molly came running through the doorway to the kitchen first. "Well, good morning, my little angels. Did you sleep well in daddy's bed?" Annie smiled as she walked to the refrigerator to grab their breakfast, thankful she had prepared their dishes the night before. She sat them on the floor and watched them devour their food.

Within moments Annie heard Sam's footsteps running down the stairs. He always ran down the stairs like a little kid. Annie grabbed a second mug from the cupboard and prepared Sam a cup of coffee.

"You must have been exhausted last night? When we came upstairs, your room was quiet, so I brought the dogs in with me. Did you have a friendly chat with Aleena?" Annie didn't know how to answer that question.

She nodded her head, "Oh yes, it was nice to chat..." Sam didn't dig any further, and Annie was thankful. It's not like she could tell Sam what Aleena thought of the two of them becoming a couple. They were already so close to sealing the deal. Annie knew words like hers would only spark an argument.

Annie wanted to avoid any further conversation about Aleena. "I am going to have myself a quick shower and unpack. I promised work I would dedicate the next few weeks to our project. So, if you need me, I'll be upstairs." Sam nodded. He was all too familiar with the current workloads. He knew they both enjoyed their time back in New York, but he too had fallen behind on his work.

CHAPTER 27

The Unexpected Phone Call

The next few months had gone by without incident. Annie and Sam had fallen back into the old routine of being no more than roommates. Annie wasn't sure if the spark had disappeared or if they were both too afraid to confront it again.

They had flown to New York on a few separate occasions so that Jersey could visit with his momma. Julee never appeared to be getting better. The head nurse told Annie, in confidence, they were still hopeful. Annie wanted her to know that Jersey was living a healthy-happy life until the day he could be with his momma again. She would snap photos as often as possible to reassure Julee.

One day, unexpectedly, Annie received a phone call. She recognized the number right away. It was Julee's number, and it was her voice on the other end. This call caught Annie off guard. Annie was always the one who reached out to Julee for the past few months. Annie's heart sank. Her mind was racing as she tried to gather her thoughts. *What if she wanted Jersey to return to New York? Would she let Jersey stay here indefinitely?* Annie knew the answer to that question. Julee's whole reason for getting better was to reunite with Jersey. *Annie, stop stalling and answer the phone.*

"Good morning Julee, how are you?"

"I am wonderful, Annie. I wanted to call and let you know that my brother Kevin and I arrived in Texas just a few hours ago. We wanted to stop and visit with you. I'll be honest, Annie. I am in full remission, and I want to bring Jersey home with me. I know you have taken great care of him for months now, but I am his momma, and he belongs with me."

Annie tried to understand the full magnitude of what Julee was saying. "You're in Murphy, Texas—right now?" She felt sick to her stomach. She knew she had to prepare for this day to come but thought she would have more time.

"Annie, I am so sorry. I know this comes as a complete shock to you, but we always knew, or should I say, hoped this day would come. We will be staying here for a week. Kevin and I have some family that lives in Dallas. We plan on visiting them and celebrating my remission."

"Let me confirm it with Sam, but I think tonight would be an excellent time for the two of you to stop over, say five o'clock? We can have dinner and discuss Jersey's future. You know the address. I will call you back if we need to change the time."

Annie ran downstairs to find Sam. The tears were flowing, at record speed. She didn't bother to wipe them away. "Sam! Sam," she cried! Annie raced around the house, calling out his name. Sam came bolting through the back door.

"Annie, are you okay? I took my laptop out onto the porch while Jersey and Molly played."

"Sam, I have some great news, Julee is in remission, she's getting better." Annie's eyes filled up with tears.

Sam wrapped his arms around Annie and hugged her as tightly as he could. "That's great news Annie, so why are you crying?" Annie sobbed in his arms for what seemed like an eternity before she could tell him what was happening.

"Julee, and Kevin are in town, and they are coming to take Jersey!" Annie cried even harder. Hearing her own words made it seem more real, somehow.

"Okay, Annie, calm down. I know you love Jersey but we both know that he belongs with his momma. Jersey is not ours to keep. You knew that when we brought him here."

Annie knew Sam was right. Of course, they wanted Julee to go into remission so Jersey could go and live with her. Annie cried harder and louder. She didn't want to lose Jersey, and what about Molly? She loved Jersey as much as they did.

Annie opened the back door and took a walk toward the pond. She left Molly and Jersey in the yard. She wanted to clear her head and come up with a plan. Annie thought hard about several scenarios. Maybe Julee would see how happy Jersey was here and allow him to stay. Annie knew that was never going to happen. *What if she moved to Texas?* Annie didn't know her financial situation, but if she could afford it, why not? Then Annie came up with her best idea yet. She raced back to the house to look for Sam and share her idea with him.

CHAPTER 28

Julee Pays a Visit

It was four- forty-five when Annie heard a vehicle driving down the road. She peeked out the window. Just as she had guessed, it was Julee with her brother Kevin. He pulled the car into the driveway. Annie and Sam walked out onto the porch to greet them.

"Julee, you look fantastic," Sam said. He wrapped his arms around her. Annie nodded her in agreement. "You do look wonderful, Julee. I am so happy you are in recovery. You fought a long hard battle."

Sam ushered the four of them into the living room. Jersey and Molly were still perched at the window—barking. Julee spotted Jersey and ran toward him. She held him in her arms and cried. "Jersey, you are the only reason I am alive today. You are my life, and I can't wait for us to be together!" Annie cried as she watched Jersey's tail wag, as he drowned his momma with kisses. He knew who she was, and Annie could see the smile on his face. Jersey was happy. He was delighted.

Sam interrupted the moment. "Dinner should be ready soon. In the meantime, Annie, why don't you take Julee out onto the porch? Kevin and I will bring out some wine, and we can enjoy the fresh air."

Kevin commented on how beautiful and peaceful it was here. Julee nodded her head in agreement. "It is a gorgeous town, and your house is lovely," Julee said with a big smile.

Julee wasn't letting Jersey out of her sight. He sat perched on her lap while they discussed the plan to reunite them. Before Julee could get too far into her plans, Annie unveiled a plan of her own.

"Julee? Sam and I had an idea we wanted to run by you before you share your plan with us, that is, if you don't mind?"

"Would you and Kevin like to stay here with us instead of the hotel? You are more than welcome here."

Julee glanced over at Kevin. She saw the hesitation in his eyes. "Annie, that is so kind of you, but we are going to decline. The hotel has already been paid for the week and we enjoy staying there."

"Well, if you change your mind, we don't mind at all." Annie tried not to let her disappointment show. She wanted Julee to see how happy Jersey was here with them before whisking him away from the home he had come to know and love.

"Annie, we will be bringing Jersey back to New York this coming weekend. He cannot stay at the hotel, but I would like to come here and visit with him if that's okay?"

"Yes, of course, anytime you want. Sam and I are buried up to our ears in work right now, so we won't be venturing out too often."

Sam glanced over at Annie. He could see the tears welling up her eyes. "Come help me in the kitchen, Annie." Annie followed him through the door silently. As they reached the kitchen and were out of sight, Sam grabbed ahold of her and hugged her. "Annie, I am so sorry. But you must remember Julee is Jersey's momma. He loves her as much as Molly loves us. It's going to be okay." Sam wiped Annie's tears as he kissed her forehead. "I love you, Annie Jones, and it's going to be okay." Annie smiled. Sam hadn't called her that in quite a while. It always brought a smile to her face.

"Let's get back outside before they think we abandoned them."

The rest of the evening was quite enjoyable. Annie tried not to think about Jersey moving away or how it was going to affect them all. Julee was an amazing momma and Annie felt guilty for trying so desperately to hang on. A few hours had passed with Sam's good cooking and enjoyable conversation. Julee was the first to stand up from the table. She grabbed a few of the dishes and headed for the back door, Annie followed behind her.

"This has been such a pleasant evening, Annie. Thank you so much for everything you have done for me and Jersey."

Annie smiled. "It has been our pleasure."

Julee poked her head out the door and called Kevin. "We really must be going. It has been a long day and I am wiped out!" Kevin quickly stood up from the table, and Sam followed behind him.

Sam and Annie walked them to the door to say their goodbyes and made plans to visit with them over the next few days.

CHAPTER 29

Julee has a Change of Heart

The week was flying past. Annie refused to spend what time she had left, with Jersey, feeling sorry for herself. She made sure she gave him as much attention and love as she could.

Then it happened, while Annie and Sam were snuggled, on the couch with Molly and Jersey alongside of them, her phone rang. Annie looked at the number before answering. It was Julee. "Hi Julee, I wasn't expecting to hear from you. Is everything okay?"

Julee's voice was whispered, and Annie could hardly hear her. "Julee, honey, I can barely hear you, is everything okay?"

Annie glanced over at Sam who had the same puzzled look on his face.

Julee began speaking again, it sounded as though she had

been crying. "Annie, you have done so much for us already and I am ashamed to even be asking for a such huge favor."

Annie covered the phone, repeating to Sam what Julee had said. He was as confused as she was.

"As I was saying," continued Julee. "Kevin and I have had a chance to do a lot of talking. I love my brother don't get me wrong, but other than him living in New York, there is nothing there for me anymore. We have family, here in Texas. They live close by, and we have had the chance to visit on a few occasions. I am sorry Annie, I'm babbling. Let me get right to the point. I want to buy a home here, in Texas, for Jersey and me. A home where we can have a backyard and walk down the side of the road. A place where I can have a garden."

"What a wonderful idea Julee! Do you need Sam and I to help you do some house hunting?"

"Not exactly, Annie. The favor is much bigger than that. I would like to know if Jersey and I could stay with you until we found our house?"

Annie stood up from the couch. She was jumping up and down whispering to Sam what Julee had said.

"Absolutely, you and Jersey can stay with us as long as you would like! We have an extra bedroom, and we'll have it all set up for you when you come!"

"Annie, thank you so much! Do you need to check with Sam first," asked Julee?

"Sam is right here with me, and he is nodding his head yes. The more the merrier, he says."

"We can make all of the arrangements tomorrow, have a good night, Julee. Jersey sends his love."

Annie snapped a picture of Jersey and Molly cuddled up on the couch and instantly sent it to Julee.

"I had not expected that to happen Sam, not in a million years."

"You see Annie Jones, sometimes things just work out. You just need to have faith."

"Come here, Annie Jones, I think you need a hug. Annie plopped down on the couch and sat beside her best friend in the entire world. She curled herself into Sam's arms and snuggled up to his warm body. Sam bent his head down, kissing her on the forehead. Annie's body responded. *I want you so badly Sam, I want you to make love to me now!* Annie didn't give Sam's lips a chance to move away. She pulled him to her and with her mouth wide open, she let every emotion escape her.

At first Sam looked confused. "Are you sure this is what you want?" Sam whispered into her ear. Annie nodded her head as she led Sam's hands up and down her body. She was on fire! Sam's hands were replaced by his lips as he moved along her breasts.

Annie shivered with every soft kiss that touched her skin. "Sam, I love you and I have wanted this for so long, please make love to me!" Sam didn't hesitate. Within moments his body was pressed against hers. Annie moaned loudly as she felt her body explode, Sam's body reacted in such a way that Annie exploded over and over until her short breaths were no more than a whimper. Their bodies were drenched with sweat as they collapsed.

"Marry me, Sam," Annie blurted! Sam laughed out loud, "Are you kidding me right now Annie Jones, you are the love of my life! If I could marry you tonight, I would!

* Thank you for reading Jersey's Unexpected Arrival. I hope you will continue to follow Annie and Molly in their journeys. *

You may also like:

Annie Jones And The Animal Sanctuary (Annie Meets Molly)

https://www.facebook.com/TamisBookNook
http://bit.ly/TamiColbyBooks
https://www.instagram.com/tamisbooknook
https://tamisbooknook.wixsite.com/tamicolby